## "Marry me."

The words stunned

"I'll go back to Phoe have this baby togeth

"How can you move? You're mayor of Cedar Creek. And what if after the baby's born, I get transferred?"

"There's plenty of time for us to figure that out." He brushed his mouth over hers. "I won't lie to you. I love this town. But it can't patch the hole in my heart these past three years. You're the only one who can do that. You and our baby."

She was in a daze. She'd driven to her old hometown hoping to work out a custody agreement. Not accept a marriage proposal.

But Gabe was giving her no time to think. He lowered her to the bed and rid her of her clothes. When he shot her that grin of his, her hormones took off again, and this time they catapulted her straight out of confusion and into lust.

They'd made a mistake the last time around. As he kissed her, she suddenly didn't care. If this was a mistake, she'd make it again...and again.

* * *

**AMERICAN HEROES:**
**They're coming home—and finding love!**

Dear Reader,

I always marvel how small incidents or chance meetings can change the entire course of your life. That happened to me years ago when, just a week before I was supposed to leave for graduate school, I sat down at a lunch counter next to an air force recruiter. After some serious negotiations and hurried paperwork, I headed for officer training school instead. Absolutely one of the best decisions of my life!

So I had great fun incorporating both the air force and a chance meeting in *The Captain's Baby Bargain*. Unlike me, though, Captain Suzanne Hall has to do some serious soul-searching before she and her ex-husband, Gabe, can come to grips with the consequences of their unexpected encounter. Hope you enjoy reading their story as much as I did writing it.

All my best,

*Merline Lovelace*

# The Captain's Baby Bargain

Merline Lovelace

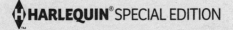
HARLEQUIN® SPECIAL EDITION

Recycling programs
for this product may
not exist in your area.

ISBN-13: 978-1-335-46589-4

The Captain's Baby Bargain

Copyright © 2018 by Merline Lovelace

**Printed in U.S.A.**

A career Air Force officer, **Merline Lovelace** served
at bases all over the world. When she hung up her
uniform for the last time, she decided to try her hand
at storytelling. Since then, more than twelve million
copies of her books have been published in over thirty
countries. Check her website at merlinelovelace.com or
friend Merline on Facebook for news and information
about her latest releases.

### Books by Merline Lovelace

### Harlequin Special Edition

#### *American Heroes*

*Marry Me, Major*

#### *Three Coins in the Fountain*

*"I Do"...Take Two!*
*Third Time's the Bride*
*Callie's Christmas Wish*

### Harlequin Romantic Suspense

### *Course of Action* (with Lindsay McKenna)

*Course of Action*
*Crossfire*
*The Rescue*

### Harlequin Desire

*The Paternity Proposition*
*The Paternity Promise*

#### *Duchess Diaries*

*Her Unforgettable Royal Lover*
*The Texan's Royal M.D.*
*The Diplomat's Pregnant Bride*
*A Business Engagement*

Visit the Author Profile page
at Harlequin.com for more titles.

To the one, the only, the handsomest,
the smartest, the kindest, the... Well, you get
the idea. There's no one like you, my darling.
Thanks for all these years of love and laughter.

And special thanks to my sister-in-arms,
the inestimable Lindsay McKenna,
for her firefighting expertise and advice.

## Chapter One

"Helluva bash, Swish."

Captain Suzanne Hall, call sign Swish, acknowledged the compliment from her former squadron mate by raising the dew-streaked bottle that had come as a "beer-in-a-bag." She'd never tried this Dutch import before. Then again, that was the whole point of the mystery bag.

"Thanks, Dingo."

The ex-military cop tipped his beer to hers while keeping an arm looped around the shoulders of the woman next to him. Personally, Swish thought the hold was more possessive than cozy. With good reason. The moment Dingo had walked in with the long-legged, *extremely* well-endowed showgirl, every male in the place had locked onto her like a heat-seeking missile.

To her credit, Chelsea Howard had ignored the

goggle-eyed stares and only occasionally put up a hand to twirl a strand of her rainbow-hued hair. "I've never been to a place like this," she commented as her gaze roamed the fun-and-games indoor-outdoor restaurant.

Neither had Swish. Lively, laughing groups sat elbow-to-elbow at picnic tables or clustered around fire pits or swapped after-work horror stories with coworkers at high tops arranged in conversational squares. Others conducted raucous battles at miniature golf or bean-bag bingo or darts or skeeball. A four-piece band thumped out country-western crossover, carrying over the clink of cutlery and buzz of conversation. In a separate section well away from the happy-hour crowd, families enjoyed the same fun atmosphere. There was a third section, a glass-enclosed, sit-down, linen-on-the-table restaurant for those more serious about eating than fun and games.

What made the whole complex so amazing, though, was the menu! Swish had almost drooled over the pictures online. Appetizers included pretzels and provolone fondue. Homemade chips with a deservedly world-famous onion dip. Cheddar and potato pierogis. BBQ pork belly nachos. Thai chili chicken wings. The dinner menu was equally exotic, but even without the rave reviews from previous guests, Swish had decided The Culinary Dropout was the perfect spot for this year's Badger Bash.

The annual Bash took place whenever two or more troops who'd served under Colonel Mike Dolan, call sign Badger, happened to be in the same general vicinity at the same time. Since Swish and two additional Badger protégées were currently stationed at Luke Air Force Base, located some miles to the west of Phoenix, they'd opted to hold the reunion here. Eight more of their former squadron mates had flown or driven in from other locales.

And since the once stag-only Bash had expanded to include spouses and/or dates, Swish had insisted on adding some couth to the event. Or, at least, ramping it up from previous years' venues. Like the New Orleans "gentlemen's" club where the performers all turned out to be drag queens. And the wolf- and moose-head decorated bar in Minot, North Dakota, that they'd had to shovel their way out of after a late May blizzard. And the off-off-the-Strip Vegas lounge featuring really bad Dean Martin and Frank Sinatra wannabes. Then there was last year's gathering at the Cactus Café, a smoke-filled dive on Albuquerque's old Route 66.

Although…even reeking of spilled beer and stale sweat, the Cactus Café had produced at least one unexpectedly happy surprise in the person of the brown-eyed blonde currently sitting across the table from Swish. At last year's Bash, Alexis Scott had walked smack up to Major Ben Kincaid, call sign Cowboy, and offered him a fat wad of cash to marry her. Ben had turned down the money but accepted the proposal. And damned if he didn't now act even more stupid about his wife than Dingo did about his showgirl. Of course, the fact that Alex was pregnant might have something to do with Ben's goofy grin.

"Where do you suppose they came up with the name Culinary Dropout?" Alex mused as she sipped her club soda and soaked up the ambiance.

"No idea." Swish speared a chunk of lobster from another appetizer, this one served in an old-fashioned glass canning jar. "Maybe the genius who created these succulent delights decided he didn't need culinary instructors to unleash his artistry."

"If that's the case, I agree with him!"

"Yo, Dingo!" The call came from a sandy-haired communications officer seated near the middle of their long table. "You think you can still hit a target?"

"Blindfolded and backwards," the former military cop turned electronics engineer drawled.

"With a bean bag?"

"Blindfolded and…"

"Ha!" His challenger clambered off his stool. "You're on!"

Chelsea went with Dingo to cheer him on. Hips rolling, her lithe body a symphony of long-legged grace, she once again popped half the eyes in the place out of their sockets.

Alex noted her best friend's impact on the crowd with a wry smile. Cowboy with unfeigned admiration. Swish with a sigh.

"I wish I could believe it was the hair," she murmured.

"Trust me," Alex answered with a laugh. "It's not the hair. Or the legs or the boobs or that wicked smile. I roomed with the woman for two years before I left Vegas for Albuquerque. Chelsea is…"

She circled a hand in the air a few times. Grinning, her husband supplied the answer.

"Chelsea."

"Exactly. And now I have to pee," she announced, easing off the high-backed stool. "Again. Good thing I didn't go through all this the first time I became a mother. I might've thought twice about this pregnancy business."

Although that might've sounded strange to an outsider, everyone at the table knew Alex had adopted her deceased sister's stepdaughter. Correction. She *and* Ben had adopted the seven-year-old. The little girl had subsequently charmed everyone in their wide circle of friends.

"How is Maria?" Swish asked.

"Smart. Stubborn. Independent. Developing an attention span that lasts about five seconds longer than your average flea." Alex patted the mound of her tummy. "And sooo excited about having a baby sister or brother."

"You don't know which yet?"

"Don't want to."

The smile she shared with her husband started a slow ache under Swish's ribs, one she'd been so damned sure she'd finally vanquished.

"That's half the wonder," Alex said softly. "Not knowing and being so totally in love with this little somebody anyway."

The ache lingered as Swish watched Alexis thread her way through the crowd toward the ladies' room. Ben tracked his wife's progress with a look that twisted the knife even more.

Dropping her gaze, Swish poked a finger at the little pile of maple-roasted wannabe nuts on the napkin in front of her. The music and laughter and thunk of beanbags hitting targets faded. The strings of lights blurred as her thoughts narrowed, turned inward, and summoned the image of a face she knew as well as her own.

*Her* husband had looked at her like Ben did his wife. Back when she'd had a husband.

She played with the wannabe nuts as the memories

crept in. Of she and Gabe growing up together in the same small Oklahoma town. Of how they'd progressed from fifth-grade puppy love to high school sweethearts to being an inseparable couple through all four years at the University of Oklahoma.

They'd married the day after graduation. The same day they'd been commissioned as Air Force second lieutenants. Then spent the next five years juggling short-notice deployments, assignments to separate bases and increasingly strained long-distance communications. Their divorce had become final three years ago, on their sixth wedding anniversary.

The hole in Swish's heart was still there but shrinking a little more each day. That's what she told herself, anyway, until Ben—who'd known them both, had been friends with them both—took advantage of the band's break between numbers to share a quiet confidence.

"I talked to Gabe last week."

"Yeah? He call you or did you call him?"

Dammit! She wished the words back as soon as they were out of her mouth. What difference did it make who initiated the conversation? Divorce was hard enough without expecting your friends to take sides and remain loyal to just one of the injured parties.

"He called me." Ben circled his beer on The Culinary Dropout's distinctive coaster. When he looked up at her again, his blue eyes were shaded. "To tell me he's thinking about getting married again."

Swish swallowed. Deep and hard. Then forced a shrug that felt as though it ripped the cartilage from her shoulder blades. "It's been three years."

She dug deeper and managed a smile. "I'm surprised he's held out this long. Last time I talked to my mom, she said every unattached female under sixty in our hometown was after him. Did Gabe mention which one snagged the prize?"

"No."

"Oh, well. No matter, I guess."

*Unless it's Alicia Johnson.*

The nasty thought plowed into her head like a runaway troop carrier. Gritting her teeth, Swish jammed on the mental brakes. She had no right to question Gabe's choice for a second trip down the aisle. Absolutely none! Even if Alicia was a pert, bubbly pain in the ass.

"He called from California," Ben was saying.

"California? What's he's doing out there?"

"Someone died. A great aunt, I think he said. He had to go out to settle her estate."

"Aunt Pat? Oh, no!"

The regret was sharp, instant, and so, so painful. She'd lost more than Gabe in the divorce. She'd lost his family, as well. They'd sided with him, of course, after the ugly details surfaced. She didn't blame them, but she'd missed his folks and his sisters and their families. And his feisty old aunt, who could spout the most incredibly imaginative oaths when the spirit moved her.

"He's driving back to Oklahoma from San Diego," Ben related. "If the timing's right, he might stop in Albuquerque to meet Alex and Maria. I told him we'd be home late tomorrow afternoon." He paused, his eyes holding hers. "Unless something unexpected came up."

"Like me throwing a world class hissy fit about you consorting with the enemy?"

"Is he? The enemy?"

Her breath left on a sigh. "No, of course not. Gabe's your friend, too. You don't have to take sides or choose between us." She hesitated several painful beats. "Did he, uh, ask about me?"

"No."

Disgusted by the hurt that generated, Swish gave herself a swift, mental kick. For God's sake! She was a captain in the United States Air Force. A combat engineer with two rotations to Iraq and one to Afghanistan under her belt. She'd built or blown up everything from runways to bridges. Yet here she was, moping like a schoolgirl who hadn't been asked to the dance because her ex chose to get on with his life.

"Well," she said briskly, "if you and Gabe do connect in Albuquerque tomorrow, tell him I wish him the best."

"Will do."

"Great. Now why don't we see how Dingo's doing blindfolded and backward?"

As one of the organizers of this year's Bash, Swish was among the last to leave when The Culinary Dropout finally closed its doors at 2:00 a.m. Even then, she provided taxi service to one of her buddies who'd flown in for the occasion.

She hung with him at his hotel room for a while, sharing black coffee and memories of the legendary Special Ops colonel who'd spawned their annual Badger Bash. She'd worked for Colonel Dolan only once, when she was a brand-new second lieutenant. The colonel could blister the paint off you with a single glance and did *not* suffer fools gladly. But Swish had learned more about leadership and taking care of her troops from him than from any of her bosses since.

Dawn was starting to streak the sky above the Superstition Mountains when she strolled out of the hotel and clicked the locks of the Thunderbird soft-top convertible she'd treated herself to when she got promoted to captain. She stood beside the merlot-colored sports car for a moment, breathing in the scent of honeysuckle and piñon while debating whether to put down the top.

The fact that she was wearing the traditional Badger Bash "uniform of the day" decided her. The generally accepted attire included boots, jeans and T-shirts sporting whatever quirky message the attendees wanted to impart. Swish had opted for a black, body-sculpting tank with a whiskered, green-eyed tiger draped over one shoulder. It had been designed and handcrafted by Ben's wife, who insisted the tiger's eyes were the exact same jungle-green as Swish's. The matching ball cap sported the same glittering black-and-gold-tiger stripes and caught her shoulder-length blond hair back into a ponytail. The perfect ensemble for tooling through a soft Arizona dawn, she decided.

Mere moments later she had the top down and the T-bird aimed for the on-ramp to I-10. Luke AFB was a good thirty miles west of Scottsdale. The prospect of a long drive didn't faze her. Having learned her lesson from previous Bashes, she'd arranged to have the rest of the weekend off. She could cruise through the dim, still-cool dawn, hit her condo, shower off the residue of the night and crash.

But first, she realized after only about fifteen miles, she had to make a pit stop. She shouldn't have downed that last cup of coffee, dammit. For another few miles she tried the bladder control exercises she'd resorted to while operating at remote sites with only the most primitive facilities.

But when she spotted a sign indicating a McDonald's at the next exit, she gave up the struggle. Flipping on the directional signal, she took the ramp for Exit 134. The iconic golden arches gleamed a little more than a block from where she got off.

Unfortunately, a red light separated her from imminent relief. She braked to a stop and drummed her fingers on the wheel. She might've been tempted to run the light if not for the vehicle stopped across the deserted intersection. It was a pickup. One of those muscled-up jobbies favored by farmers and ranchers. Older than most, though. And vaguely familiar. Narrowing her eyes, she squinted and tried to see past the headlights spearing toward her in the slowly brightening dawn.

Suddenly, her heart lurched. Stopped dead. Kicked back to life with a painful jolt.

Locking her fists on the wheel, Swish gaped at the cartoon depicted on the pickup's sloping hood. She recognized the needle-nosed insect dive-bombing an imaginary target. She should; she'd painted it herself.

Her gaze jerked from the hood to the cab. The headlights' glare blurred the driver's features. Not enough to completely obscure them, however.

Oh, God! That was Gabe. Her Gabe.

Fragments of the conversation with Cowboy rifled through her shock. California. A funeral. Gabe driving home. Visiting with Cowboy and his wife in Albuquerque.

Her precise, analytical engineer's mind made the instant connection. Phoenix sat halfway between San Diego and Albuquerque. A logical place to stop for the night, grab some sleep, break up the long drive. The not-as-precise section of her brain remained so numb with surprise that she didn't react when the light turned green. Her knuckles white, she gripped the wheel and kept her foot planted solidly on the brake.

The pickup didn't move, either. With no other traffic transiting the isolated intersection, the two vehicles sat facing each other as the light turned yellow, then red again. The next time it once again showed green, the pickup crossed the short stretch of pavement and pulled up alongside her convertible.

The driver's side window whirred down. A tanned elbow hooked on the sill. The deep baritone that used to belt out the hokiest '50s-era honky-tonk tear-jerkers rumbled across the morning quiet.

"Hey, Suze."

He'd never used her call sign in nonoperational situations. The military had consumed so much of their lives that Gabe wouldn't let it take their names, too. That attitude, Swish reflected, was only one of the many reasons he'd left the Air Force and she hadn't.

She craned her neck, squinting up from her low-slung sports car. "Hey yourself, Gabe."

"I thought I was hallucinating there for a minute. What're you doing in Phoenix?"

"I live here. I'm stationed at Luke."

"Oh, yeah? Since when?"

The fact that he didn't even know where she lived hurt. More than she would ever admit.

Swish, on the other hand, had subtly encouraged her mother to share bits of news about her former son-in-law's life since he'd moved back to Oklahoma. Mary Jackson had passed on the news that the high school tennis team Gabe coached had won state honors. And she gushed over the fact that the voters of their small hometown elected him mayor by a landslide. Somehow, though, her mom had neglected to mention the fact that Cedar Creek's mayor was getting married again.

"I've been at Luke a little over four months," Swish answered with as much nonchalance as she could muster, then let her gaze roam the dusty, dented pickup. "I see you're still driving Ole Blue."

He unbent his elbow and patted the outside of his door. "I rebuilt the engine a last year. Spins like a top."

"Mmm-hmm."

The memories didn't creep in this time. They hit like a sledgehammer.

Swish had surrendered her virginity in Ole Blue's cab. Impatiently. Hungrily. Almost angrily. She'd teased and tormented Gabe until he finally toppled her backward on the cracked leather seat and yanked down her panties. Even then, as wild with hunger as they both were, he'd been gentle. For the first few thrusts. Once past the initial startled adjustment, Swish had picked up the rhythm and climaxed mere moments later, as though she'd only been waiting for his touch to ignite those white-hot sensations.

She'd still been floating back to earth when he pulled out of her and started swearing. At himself. At her. At the incredible stupidity of what they'd just done. What if her parents found out he'd violated their trust as well as their daughter? What if he'd let himself come and gotten her pregnant! What about her scholarship to OU? The bridges she wanted to build. The exotic lands they both wanted to travel to!

Still soaring on that sexual high, Swish had kissed and stroked and nipped the cords in his neck until he cursed again, shoved the key in the ignition and drove her home.

Other, less sensual memories involving Ole Blue swirled like a colorful kaleidoscope. The night they spread an air mattress in the truck bed and stretched out to watch a gazillion stars light up the sky. The times they'd pulled into a space at the only still-operating drive-in movie in the area to munch popcorn and watch the latest action flick. The load of manure they'd loaded and hauled to fertilize the garden belonging to a friend of his mother.

A flash of headlights in the rearview mirror yanked her from the past to the present. They were still blocking the intersection, with Ole Blue hunched like an oversize panther beside Swish's red mouse of a car.

She glanced in the mirror, back at Gabe. "Well, I guess…"

"Why don't we get a cup of coffee?" He hooked his thumb at the golden arches behind him. "I obviously need to catch up on your career moves."

She opened her mouth to refuse. The memories she'd just flashed through were too raw, too painful. She'd be a fool to resurrect any more. Then again, she *did* have to make a pit stop. Like reeeeally bad now.

"Okay," she heard herself say. "I'll meet you inside… after I hit the head."

She cornered into the parking lot, killed the engine and was out of the T-bird before Ole Blue had made a U-turn at the intersection. This early in the morning the ladies' room was empty and clean as a whistle, with the pungent tang of disinfectant taking precedence over the scent of deep-fried hash browns and sausage coming from the kitchen.

When she emerged, she found Gabe lounging against a booth with a coffee cup in either hand. A smile crinkled the squint lines at the corners of his hazel eyes as he tipped his chin toward the restroom she'd just vacated.

"You must've been on the road for a while if your iron-bladder exercises failed you."

"Hey! I made it, didn't I?"

Anyone overhearing the exchange would've wondered at the subject matter. Or assumed she and Gabe shared a history that included an intimate knowledge of each other's bodily functions. Which they did.

Feeling like a total idiot for mourning the loss of that particular history, Swish reached out a hand. "Which coffee is mine?"

"Take your pick." He held out both cups. "They're the same."

She blinked, startled. Her husband had always been a two-sugars-one-cream kind of guy. "When did you start drinking undoctored coffee?"

"When I added too many extra inches to my waistline."

Her gaze made a quick up and down. If Gabe had put on extra inches, she sure as hell couldn't see them. The chest covered by his stretchy black T-shirt tapered to a still-trim waist. The snug jeans emphasized his flat belly. His lean hips. The hard, muscled thighs she'd traced so often with her hands and her mouth and her...

"You sure you don't want more than coffee?" he asked, gesturing to the illuminated menu. "I'll be happy to stand you to a Number 3."

The fact that he remembered her preference for a Big Breakfast with Hotcakes made her throat ache. "This is good," she murmured, sliding into the booth he'd staked out.

The silence that followed was short but awkward. And obviously painful, as they both rushed to break it.

"What are you…?"

"So sorry about…"

They both broke off, and he gestured for her to go on.

"So sorry to hear about Aunt Pat. What happened?"

"An aortic aneurism. She died in her sleep. One of her spin-class buddies found her the next morning."

Swish wasn't surprised that the feisty seventy-six-year-old had been into spinning along with all her other fitness pursuits. She and Pat had once run side by side in a 5k Race for the Cure with the older woman decked out in flashing sneakers, cotton-candy-pink leggings and a cropped tank that announced she was One Fast Oldie.

"How's your mom taking her sister's death?"

"Hard. She flew out for the funeral but couldn't stay to help settle the estate. Her hip's been giving her trouble."

The reply plucked at Swish's hurt again. She'd been so close to his family. His dad before he died, his mom, his sisters. To cover the ache, she switched subjects.

"*My* mom told me about the election. Ninety-four percent of the vote. Pretty impressive for a high school history teacher-slash-tennis coach."

"Yeah, well…"

The grin that had haunted her dreams for too many months slipped out. As self-deprecating and sexy as she remembered. She felt its all-too-familiar impact wrap around her heart.

"Hard to bask in the glow of victory when my cousins constitute at least half the electorate."

Swish had to laugh. "I know most of those cousins.

They're as stubborn and hardheaded as you are, Mr. Mayor. They wouldn't have voted for you unless they believed in you."

"Maybe. Or it might've been because I ran against Dave Forrester."

Her jaw dropped. "You're kidding! Freckle-faced Forrester overcame his shyness enough to run for public office?"

"Freckle-faced Forrester now owns the largest oil and gas franchise in the county," Gabe returned drily. "Lucky for me—but not for my constituents—he's been slapped with a half-dozen lawsuits for property damage due to fracking. He's not the most popular guy around Cedar Creek these days."

Wow! The skinny, gap-toothed kid who'd traded spitballs with her? An oil and gas executive? She was still trying to get her head around that when Gabe broke into her thoughts.

"What about you? What are you doing at Luke?"

She shook off the tendrils of her past and leaped gratefully into the present. "I'm assigned to the 56th Fighter Wing. Would you believe I head up the Base Emergency Engineer Response team?"

"Prime BEEF? Now I'm impressed."

The designation didn't begin to describe the scope of her team's duties. The mission of Luke AFB was to train the men and women who flew and maintained the F-16 Fighting Falcon and the F-35 Lightning, the world's newest and most sophisticated fighter. The base population included more than ten thousand active duty, reserve and civilian personnel, plus their families. Another seventy thousand retirees lived in the local area. Swish's job was to make sure the facilities were in place to support all these people in both peacetime and wartime.

"That's quite a responsibility," Gabe commented. "It's what you trained for. What you've worked so hard for. And why you were awarded that Bronze Star after your last deployment."

"You know about the Bronze Star?"

She couldn't keep the surprise out of her voice. He couldn't keep the bite out of his.

"Know that my wife…?" He stopped. Took a breath. Started again. "Know that my *former* wife and her team risked their lives to repair an abandoned runway outside Mosul? That they opened the airstrip despite heavy enemy fire so US aircraft could use it as a base to repel an ISIS attack? Yeah, I know about it."

Okay, that gave her a warm buzz. Almost warm enough to mitigate the fact that he hadn't known she was now assigned to Luke. Not quite warm enough to erase the news Ben had imparted last night, though. She looked down at her now sludgy coffee. Looked up. Took her courage in both hands.

"Cowboy told me you're getting married again."

"I'm thinking about it."

"Anyone I know?"

He hesitated, shrugged. "Alicia Johnson."

*Dammit all to hell!*

Somehow, someway, she managed to keep from crushing her cup and slopping coffee over the table. A bitter realization stayed her hand. As much as she disliked the nauseatingly effervescent pixie, she had no right to castigate Gabe for his choice of partners. God knows, he hadn't castigated her when she turned to someone else out of desperate loneliness.

"Whatever you decide," she got out, despite lungs squeezed so tight she could hardly breath, "I hope you find the 'forever' we were so sure we had."

He stretched out a hand, covered hers. "Same goes, Susie Q."

It was the silly nickname that did it. His pet name for her from the fifth grade on. Forever associated in both of their minds with the package of cream-filled chocolate cupcakes she'd brought to his bedroom when he fell out of a tree and broke his collarbone.

She tried, she really tried, to keep her smile from wobbling. Twisting her hand, she gave his what she intended as a companionable squeeze. His fingers threaded through hers. So strong. So warm. So achingly familiar.

He raised their joined hands. Brought the back of hers to his lips. Brushed a kiss across her knuckles. Once. Twice. Swish didn't even *try* to pull away.

Until he gently, slowly, lowered his hand and eased it out of hers.

## Chapter Two

"I...uh..."

Gabe smothered a curse as his wife—his *former* wife!—stammered and tried to shrug off the impact of their brief contact.

One touch. One friggin' touch, and she looked ready to bolt. He should let her. God knew it wouldn't be the first time. Instead, he soothed her obvious nervousness with a safe, neutral topic.

"I didn't get to talk to Cowboy much over the phone. It sounded like he's enjoying his foray into fatherhood, though."

"He is."

She relaxed, bit by almost imperceptible bit, and Gabe refused to analyze the relief that ripped through him. He'd think about it later. Along with the ache in his gut just sharing a booth with her generated.

"Did you know his wife, Alex, designs glitzy tops and accessories for high-end boutiques?"

"No." He gestured toward the tiger draped over her shoulder. "Did she design that?"

"She did."

"Nice."

*Very* nice. Although…

Now that he'd recovered from the shock of their unexpected meeting, Gabe wasn't sure he liked the changes he saw in the woman sitting opposite him. She was older. That went without saying. But she'd lost weight in the three years since they'd said their final goodbye. Too much weight. She'd always been slim. With a waist he could span with his hands and small, high breasts that never required a bra when she wasn't in uniform. Now her cheekbones slashed like blades across her face and that sparkly, stretchy black tank showed hollows where her neck joined her shoulders.

And those lines at the corners of her eyes. Gabe knew most of them came from the sun. And from squinting through everything from high-tech surveying equipment to night-vision goggles. But the lines had deepened, adding both maturity and a vulnerability that tugged at protective instincts he'd thought long buried.

The eyes themselves hadn't changed, though. Still a deep, mossy green. And still framed by lashes so thick and dark she'd never bothered with mascara. The hair was the same, too. God, how he loved that silvery, ash-blond mane. She'd worn it in a dozen different styles during all their years together. The feathery cut that made her look like a sexy Tinker Bell. The chin-sweeping bob she'd favored in high school. The yard-long spill she'd sported in college. How many times had he tunneled his fingers through that satin-smooth waterfall? A hundred? Two?

He liked the way she wore it now, though. Long enough to pull through the opening at the back of her ball cap, just long enough for the ends to cascade over her right shoulder. Gabe had to curl his hands into fists to keep from reaching across the table and fingering those silky strands.

He sipped his coffee, instead, and tried his damnedest to maintain an expression of friendly interest as she brought him up to date on other mutual friends. Pink, getting ready to ship across the pond again. Dingo and the showgirl he'd been seeing off and on for over a year now. A real wowzer, if even half of the adjectives Suze used to describe the buxom brunette were true. Cowboy's wife, Alex, expanding her clothing design business even faster than they were expanding their family.

Strange, Gabe thought. He always associated their friends with their call signs. Yet he never thought of Suze as Swish. There were several different explanations of how she'd acquired that tag. One version held it resulted from the detailed analysis she'd sketched on a scrap of paper during a fierce, intrasquadron basketball game. In swift, decisive strokes she'd demonstrated the correct amount of thrust and proper parabolic arc to swish in a basket.

Another version was that she'd gained the tag after one of her troops mired a Swiss-made bulldozer in mud. Suze reportedly climbed aboard, rocked the thirty-ton behemoth back and forth, and *swished* it out.

There was another version. One involving beer, a bet and a camel, although Suze always claimed the details were too hazy for her to remember.

Gabe knew his reluctance to use her call sign was only one small indicator of the rift that had gradually, inexorably widened to a chasm. He hadn't resented sharing her with the Air Force or with the troops she worked with. Not at first. Not until they became her surrogate family. But she always was, always would be, Suze to him.

Or *Susie Q.* The pet name came wrapped in so many layers of memories. Some innocent, like the time he broke his collarbone and she'd perched on the side of his bed to feed him bits of her cream-filled chocolate treats. And some not so innocent. Like the time…

Without warning, Gabe went tight. And hard. And hungry. Smothering another curse, he shoved the image of his wife's nipples smeared with whipped cream out of his head. But he had to drag in long, slow breaths before his blood started circulating above his waist again.

"I can't tell if Dingo's serious about Chelsea or not," Suze was saying. "He hooks up with her whenever he's in Vegas. And they spent a week together in Cabo a few months back. But neither of them seem to be talking about long term." She cocked her head. "Gabe?"

"Sorry. I was thinking of something else."

"Right."

She fiddled with the tab on the lid of her cup. They'd covered every banal topic they could while dancing away from the only one that mattered. Silence stretched between them. Gabe was reluctant to break it, and even more reluctant to end this strange interlude. Suze finally took the lead.

"Well, if you're going to make Albuquerque this evening, you probably should hit the road."

"Probably should."

"Unless…"

She flicked the tab. Up. Down. Didn't quite meet his eyes.

"Unless?" he prompted.

"Unless you'd like to swing by my place for breakfast first. It's out of your way but…" The barest hint of a smile flitted across her face. "I still can't cook worth a damn but I *have* learned to concoct a relatively passable Mexican frittata."

It was an olive branch. A tentative step toward putting the past behind them and becoming friends again. That's all it was, Gabe told himself fiercely. All it could be. Yet he snatched it with both hands.

"You're on."

Even before he snapped his seat belt and keyed Ole Blue's ignition, his thoughts had done a one-eighty. This was a mistake. Possibly one of epic proportions. There was no way in hell either of them could back to being just friends. But as Gabe trailed her maroon sports car through the now-bright Arizona morning, he came up with a dozen different explanations for his temporary insanity.

Neither of them had tried to deny that their frequent separations while they were both in uniform had created the first cracks in their marriage. The cracks had gotten wider every time Gabe suggested they choose different career paths, ones that wouldn't put them on opposite sides of the globe so often. The fissures had become a yawning crevasse when he'd issued a flat ultimatum.

Looking back, he knew he shouldn't have forced her to choose between him and the Air Force. Or hung up his uniform and headed for Oklahoma while they were still struggling to balance the deep, visceral satisfaction she got from her job with his gnawing need to get back to his roots.

And he sure as hell shouldn't have let her admission that she'd turned to someone else for comfort eat like acid on his pride. They'd been separated for six months by then. Already talking around the edges of divorce, when they talked at all.

That was when he'd heard the rumor. Third hand, passed via a friend of a friend of a friend. It hadn't meant anything, the well-meaning pal had assured him. Suzanne had already given the guy his marching orders.

Gabe knew then he should've swallowed his rage at the thought of Suzanne, *his* Suzanne, in another man's arms, jumped on a plane and tried one last time to heal the breach.

Which is exactly what he would've done if she hadn't called back while he was in the process of throwing a few things in an overnight bag. Every word icy and clipped, she'd told him she'd applied for two weeks' leave. She needed to get away. Think things through. And, like a fool, he'd let her go. Didn't ask where. Didn't try to track her down. Just stubbornly, stupidly believed deep in his heart they'd find a way back to each other. He'd continued to believe it right up until she FedExed him the divorce papers.

As the memories flashed by with the same speed as the miles, his mind went to a place he knew it shouldn't. Maybe Suze had offered more than an olive branch back there at McDonald's. Maybe these past three years had been as lonely for her as they had for him. Maybe, just maybe, she was giving him the chance to correct the most colossal blunder of his life.

If she was, and if he did, all ten levels of hell would freeze over before he let her go again.

The fierce vow probably explained why she'd barely closed the door of her condo behind them before he made his move. That, and the fact that a swift glance around her airy living room revealed no reminders of their broken marriage. Even with the wood shutters tilted against the morning sun, enough light slanted in for Gabe to see the furniture was new. So was the triple panel of bold, slashing color mounted above the sofa. Even the oversize area rug that looked like it had been woven from fabric scraps in dozens of different colors and patterns.

She must have caught his frown as he studied the rug. Tossing her keys and small clutch purse on the tiled counter that separated the living room from the kitchen, she addressed the issue head on. "I'm only renting this place until I decide where to buy."

He answered with a shrug that added an edge in her voice.

"It came furnished, so I put our Turkish…" She stopped, restarted. "So I put the Turkish carpets in storage with the rest of my things."

For some reason that deliberate midcourse correction pissed Gabe off. She couldn't admit they'd ever shared a home? Couldn't cherish the small treasures they'd collected from all over the world?

Conveniently forgetting that he'd boxed up pretty much every item he'd carted back to Oklahoma and stashed them in the attic of *his* home, Gabe forced a grin. "Seems like I remember us rolling around naked on those Turkish carpets a few times."

The surprise that flashed across her face gave him a dart of fierce satisfaction. It also provided a chance to dig the spur in a little deeper.

"More than a few times, now that I think about it. Often enough for one of us to get a little carpet burn on her ass, anyway."

When he waggled his brows, she laughed and shook her head.

"That was you, big guy. After which, you threatened to tell folks you'd been wounded in the line of duty."

"At which point *you* threatened to pin a purple heart on said wound."

"Would've served you right if I had!"

They were both grinning now, and Gabe moved in for the kill. Lifting a hand, he brushed his knuckles down her cheek. "We had some good times, didn't we?"

Her laughter faded. The twin emerald pools he'd seen himself in so many times stared up at him. Gabe waited, his heart slamming against his ribs, until her breath left on a whisper of a sigh.

"Yes, we did."

He opened his palm and cupped her chin, then feathered his thumb across her lower lip. His pulse was drumming in his ears now. And in that instant, he knew he wouldn't—*couldn't*—take Alicia up on her increasingly unsubtle hints that she was ready to move in with him. Permanently.

This was the only woman he'd ever loved. The one he'd ached for with the fumbling, frantic passion of youth. The one he'd promised to share his life with. There wasn't room in his heart for anyone but her.

"I've missed you, Suze."

"I've missed you, too." Tears dimmed the luminescent green of her eyes. "So much I hurt with it."

His palm slid to her nape. His other hand came up to ease off her ball cap. With it out of the way, he tugged at the squishy elastic band that held her hair. The wind-tangled strands came free and framed her face.

"There," he said, his voice gruff. "I've been aching to do that since the moment we walked into that McDonald's."

"Gabe…"

It was half sigh, half plea. Heat roiling in his belly, he tightened his hold on her nape.

"I've been aching to do this, too."

He fully intended to keep the kiss gentle. To stoke her hunger carefully, slowly, until it matched the fire now smoldering in his blood. But she fitted herself against him with a familiar intimacy that sparked searing pleasure at every contact point. Her mouth, her breasts, her hips. All straining against him. All filling him with a raging need that made him whip an arm around her waist and haul her even closer.

Swish reacted instinctively. The feel of him against her, of the hard press of his mouth on hers, shattered the dam. Hunger, hot and urgent, poured through her. Panting, gasping, her lungs burning, her lips frantic under his, she hooked her arms around his neck. The last shreds of sanity screamed at her to pull back. Now! While she still could! But the rest of her, every atom of the rest of her, wanted Gabe with a ferocity so intense it seared her soul.

She wasn't sure who attacked whose clothing first. She might've yanked up his black T-shirt to get at the hard, tanned muscles of his chest. Or maybe he whipped her tank top up and off. She didn't know. Didn't care. She was too busy heeling out of her half-boots to think about it.

She kicked the boots away at the same instant his hands went to the zipper of her jeans. He shoved them down over her hips. She shimmied the rest of the way out. She hadn't bothered with a bra. She never did when not in uniform. So all she had on when he scooped her up was the thin layer of her black lace hipsters.

"That way," she gasped, pointing to the arch that led to the two bedrooms. Unnecessarily, as it turned out, as Gabe was already halfway there.

The master bedroom suite echoed the same eclectic style and bright colors as the living room. Red, yellow and turquoise pillows in varying shapes accented the sage-colored comforter. The collage of desert sunrises and sunsets arranged above the headboard picked up the same colors.

Gabe didn't so much as glance at the gorgeous display. He almost dumped her on the bed and dragged off her panties before stripping off the rest his own clothes. Boots. Jeans. Jockeys.

Jaw taut, nostrils flaring, he turned back to her. His eyes, those green-brown eyes flecked with bits of gold, raked from her neck to her knees. Suze could see herself reflected in the dark irises. Her arms flung up beside her head in wild abandon. Her breasts bare, the nipples already hard and aching for his touch. Her stomach hollowing as the muscles low in her belly clenched in greedy anticipation.

Then, just as she opened her legs to welcome him, he turned away. She lay frozen, unable to move or think or understand why he reached for the jeans he'd just discarded. She whipped her arms down and pushed up on one elbow. She was all set to torch him like one of the commercial high-pressure propane flamethrowers her fire protection troops used when he faced her again, a crumpled foil packet in his hand.

"I have no idea how long I've carried this in my wallet," he said with a wry grimace. "A year maybe."

Which implied, she thought on a surge of primal satisfaction, he hadn't delved into his secret stash for prissy missy Alicia Johnson.

She dismissed as totally irrelevant the possibility that Alicia might have supplied the necessary protective measures herself. The only thing that mattered to her now was that Gabe, her Gabe, apparently hadn't *initiated* a sexual encounter.

Until now.

"Let me."

Her heart stuck in her throat, she rolled onto her knees and held out her hand. She squeezed every ounce of pleasure she could out of tearing open the packet and sheathing his now rigid erection. The veined shaft rising hard and pulsing from its nest of wiry chestnut hair triggered atavistic instincts as old as time. This was her mate. The man she'd given her heart to years before she gave him her virginity.

She'd never looked at another man during their years together. Never wanted another man's hands on her. At least, not until the hurt and the loneliness had got too much to bear. Even then, she'd taken only one other man to her bed.

The experience had left her so empty, so heartbroken that she'd never repeated it. But word had gotten back to Gabe. How, she never knew, not that it mattered. His raw fury had leaped from the email he'd sent asking if it was true.

The anger still simmered, she discovered. Not as raw. Not as livid. But she could see it in his eyes when he tunneled his hands through her hair and tipped her head back.

"Do you have any idea how many times I've thought about you doing this with someone else?" he asked, his voice low and rough.

"I can guess."

"That damned near killed me, Suze."

"I know," she said, her throat tight. "I was sorry then. I'm sorry now."

The reply did little to take the edge off his hostility. He toppled her back, splaying her on the sage-green spread, then followed her down. His body was rock hard, his muscles taut and his tendons corded as he kneed her legs apart.

She welcomed him, craving a cleansing as much as he did. Yet for all his seeming anger, he took time to make sure she was primed. His fingers found all the triggers. Started the pinwheels spinning and the juices flowing.

She didn't have to tell him that she was wet and ready. He knew her body's responses as well as she did. Better. She was panting when he positioned himself between her thighs. Groaning when she lifted her hips and rose up to meet his thrusts. She ground her mouth against his, more than matching his savage hunger.

Her climax slammed into her with almost zero warning. One moment she was straining against his hips.

The next, she arched her spine, groaned deep in her throat and exploded.

She had no idea how long she drifted on those dark, undulating waves of pleasure before she realized he was still rock hard and buried inside her. When she pried her eyes open, the worry in his green-brown eyes melted her heart.

"You okay?"

The question was as tight and strained as his body. Swish slicked her palms over his taut shoulders. "More okay than I've been in three years."

The reply didn't seem to reassure him. Still frowning, he propped himself up on his elbows and framed her face with his palms. "I didn't mean to be so rough."

"Do you hear me complaining?"

"No, but…"

"We need to get that old hurt out of our systems, Gabe. We're halfway there."

"Halfway?"

"Yep."

She gave the muscles low in her belly a tight, hard squeeze. A flush rushed into Gabe's cheeks, and she squeezed again. Reveling in his response, she rolled onto her hip, then up to her knees.

"All right, fella. My turn to get rough."

By the time they finished, Gabe felt drained of all bodily fluids and Suze lay across his chest like a bag of bones. When he eased her to the side to cradle her in the crook of his arm, she nuzzled her nose into his neck.

"Gimme a few minutes," she grunted. "Then I'll get up 'n' make you that omelet."

"No hurry. I'm good."

Christ! As if that bland adjective came anywhere close to describing how he felt at that moment.

"Okay," she muttered against his throat. "I was up all night last night. I'll just snuggle here for a little bit."

*Snuggle forever.*

Gabe caught the suggestion before it slipped out. But the words hung there in his mind as she dropped into a light doze. Not five minutes later, she was out like a brick.

That was fine with him. He wasn't on a tight schedule. School was over for the year, he wouldn't start coaching summer tennis clinics for another week and his deputy mayor could handle any minor crises that might erupt. He could lie here as long as he wanted, his wife sleeping beside him, her breath warm on his neck and the overhead fan gently stirring the ends of her hair.

He teased the loose strands with an absent, hazy concentration. They slid through his fingers, still wind-whipped but not dry or dusty. As he twisted a skein around his thumb, his thoughts segued from the familiar feel of her hair to what their unexpected encounter might mean in terms of their future.

Grimacing, he reinforced his silent decision to end things with Alicia. She'd still been stinging from her own divorce when she'd turned to Gabe for companionship. Somehow their casual encounters had morphed into dates, then to an "understanding" that Alicia had begun to take more seriously than Gabe did. She'd been pushing for them to move in together. Her place or his, she didn't care, and he'd been edging close to saying what the hell.

Now...

He scrunched a few inches to the left so he could

look down at his wife's face without going cross-eyed. He always got a kick out of watching her sleep. Those ridiculously thick lashes fanned her cheeks. Her breath soughed in and out through half-open lips. And every once in a while her nose would twitch and she'd make little snuffling noises.

God, he loved this woman! She'd been in his blood, in his heart, for almost as long as he could remember. Maybe now they could put all the hurt and separation and loneliness behind them. Maybe their chance meeting at that deserted intersection wasn't chance at all, but a…

The sudden, shrill notes of a xylophone clanged through the quiet. Gabe jerked and Suze's head popped up.

"Wha…?"

She blinked owlishly, then muttered a curse when the xylophone clanged again. Rolling onto her opposite side, she slapped her palm against the nightstand until she located her iPhone. She flopped onto her back and squinted at the screen. Evidently she recognized the number because she scowled and stabbed the talk button.

"Captain Hall," she croaked, her voice still hoarse with sleep. As she listened for a few moments, her scowl slashed into a frown. She jerked upright and gripped the phone with a white-knuckled fist.

"Casualties?"

Gabe went taut beside her. The single word brought back stark memories of his own time in the Air Force. He'd begun his career as a weapons director flying aboard the Air Force's sophisticated E3-A, the Airborne Warning and Control System. AWACS aircraft averaged hundreds of sorties a year. Flying at thirty thousand feet, they provided the "eyes in the sky" for other aircraft operating in a combat environment.

After four years in AWACS Gabe had volunteered to transition to drone operations in an effort to remain on the same continent as Suze for at least a few months out of the year. He'd been transferred to Creech Air Force Base, just outside Las Vegas, and trained to remotely pilot the MQ-9 Reaper. With its long loiter time, wide-range sensors and precision weapons, the Reaper provided a unique capability to perform conduct strikes against high-value, time-sensitive targets.

Turned out Gabe was good at jockeying that joystick. Good at locking onto even the fastest-moving targets. Good at launching his laser-guided missiles from precisely the right angle and altitude to destroy those top priority targets.

It was the secondary casualties that churned his insides. He could see them through the unblinking eyes of high-powered spy satellites. The bystanders hurled fifty or a hundred yards from the impact site. The wounded leaving trails of blood in the dirt as they crawled and begged for help. The parents keening soundlessly as they cradled children who'd run to or been hidden near the target.

Collateral damage. That was the catchall phrase for noncombatants caught in the cross fire. Gabe had never taken a shred of pride in his body count, never wanted to know the numbers. Even now he couldn't relax until he heard Suze expel a relieved breath.

"No casualties? Thank God for that. I'm on my way." She tossed aside the rumpled sheet and almost tripped over his discarded jeans on her way to her closet. "ETA twenty minutes."

She tossed the phone on the dresser and yanked open a drawer. With one leg in a pair of no-nonsense briefs, she offered a quick explanation. "Sorry, Gabe. There's been an accident. I have to get to the base."

"Aircraft?"

"Pipeline break." She dragged on a sports bra followed by the regulation brown T-shirt. "Evidently we've got the mother of all fuel spills."

Gabe knew that meant getting a hazmat team on-scene ASAP. Spilled aviation fuel was not just a fire and explosion danger, but also a potential environmental disaster. The FEMA Emergency Management course he'd attended after being elected mayor had offered some excellent tips on exactly this kind of crisis.

Tucking the sheet around his waist, he waited while Suze yanked on her desert-colored BDU pants and shirt, then plopped down on the side of the bed to pull on her socks and boots.

"I went to the FEMA Disaster Response course in Baton Rouge last month. They're recommending a new sorbent for fuel spills that…"

"Sorry, Gabe, I don't have time."

She stood up, grabbed her phone and a leather trifold he knew contained her ID, her driver's license, a credit card and some cash.

"I'll call you when I can."

He was still sitting in bed with the sheet bunched around his waist when the front door slammed behind her.

## Chapter Three

The spill was even worse than Suzanne had feared.

As the designated training base for the F-35 Joint Strike Fighter, Luke AFB had awarded a multi-million-dollar contract to a civilian construction firm to modify the aviation fuel bulk storage tanks, feed lines and manifold system. The intent was to improve the new fighter's refueling turnaround and thus increase the number of sorties that could be flown during a training cycle. Suzanne had participated in the multi-organization review and final approval of the contractor's construction plan. She'd also assigned one of her troops to monitor the construction on a daily basis.

The project had gone smoothly to date. Or so they'd thought. When she arrived at the coordination point, the quick briefing she got from Hank Butler, the Base Fire Chief, in his role as acting on-scene commander, told another story. An experienced civilian with more than thirty years of firefighting and disaster response under his belt, Butler had shared valuable tips with Swish and her team during their training exercises. He'd also worked with her on several smaller spills.

"You're gonna have your hands full with this one, Captain."

According to the chief, the contractor had breached an underground fuel line. That was bad enough. What made it worse was that the breach hadn't been detected until a ground-water monitoring well more than half a mile from the storage facility recorded significant levels of contamination. Her mind clicking a hundred miles an hour, Swish took both mental and physical notes as the chief ran through the actions taken so far.

All personnel evacuated from the fuel tank farm. Check. All feeder lines shut down. Check. All refueling and flying activity within a designated radius halted. Check. Fire and explosive potential from leaked fumes being monitored. Check.

Relieved that the most immediate danger to both people and facilities had been addressed, Swish geared up for the long, tough job ahead. Although Logistics procured and stored the fuel, the loggies shared responsibility for containing and cleaning up spills with the civil engineers. In close coordination with the EPA, of course. And the Arizona Department of Environmental Quality. And the Staff Judge Advocate. And a half-dozen other agencies and concerned parties.

Right now her most pressing priorities were to first locate the breach in the underground line, then block further flow into the groundwater. Thankfully, every member of her Spill Response Team had trained for just such emergencies. Several had experience with similar incidents. One, thank God, had been part of the Luke AFB team that identified hazardous waste sites resulting from disposal methods that were approved back in the '50s and '60s but didn't meet modern EPA standards.

Mike Gentry was a bioenvironmental engineer and key member of her Spill Response Team. Almost as senior as the fire chief, Mike had been talking retirement. Swish could only murmur a fervent prayer of thanks that he'd held off—although this mess might well convince him to put in his papers sooner rather than later.

"Okay, Mike, with the feeder line shut down, we can use reports from monitoring wells along the line to help pinpoint the leak, right?"

"Right. I've already requested immediate status reports from wells eleven and twelve, Captain."

Using hard data from the monitoring wells and on-site samples, they pinpointed the probable point of the leak. Swish's heart twisted when she drove out to the site and surveyed the greasy oil slick on the long, narrow lake. The scorching May heat didn't help the situation. With the afternoon temperature nudging close to a hundred degrees, toxic fumes danced with heat waves to form shimmering, iridescent clouds above the water's surface. Breathing heavily through her respirator, Swish knew a single spark could set the whole damned lake on fire.

Sweat poured down her temples and stung her eyes, making each breath she sucked in through the respirator a Herculean chore, but she didn't remove the mask until the booms were in place, the skimmer operating.

* * *

It was midafternoon when Swish grabbed a few minutes to scarf down the sandwiches and chips that Food Service personnel delivered to her and the rest of the team. Close to seven in the evening, she finally took a long enough break to call Gabe. Stepping away from the dig area, she thumbed her contacts listing. His cell phone number was still there. Even after all this time apart, she hadn't been able to bring herself to delete it. She had no idea if it was still good but tried it anyway.

"Hey, Suze," he answered after a few rings. "Got everything under control?"

"More or less." Puzzled, she cocked her head. "I'm hearing a funny buzz. Where are you?"

"Cruising along in Ole Blue."

A figure waved to her. Holding up her index finger, she pantomimed "Be right with you" to the EPA rep who'd been sweating alongside her and her team all afternoon.

"Cruising where?" she asked, her gaze on the excavation in progress.

"Home."

The succinct reply jerked Swish back to the conversation. "Home, like in Oklahoma?"

"Roger that."

She tried not to feel hurt. But she did, dammit. She did. "Nice of you to take off without bothering to say goodbye."

"I left a note."

Now she wasn't just hurt. She was pissed. "Oh. Well. That's okay, then. A note makes you rolling out of my bed and hitting the road without a word just fine and dandy."

"Christ, Suze!" A matching anger rolled back at her.

"What the hell did you expect me to do? Sit around for two or three days, twiddling my thumbs until you remembered you left a husband in that bed?"

"*Ex*-husband."

"Yeah," he snapped, "and that's pretty much the reason why."

She couldn't believe he was ripping at her for doing her job! Okay, she should've called sooner. But she was damned if she'd apologize or, worse, grovel. She'd done both often enough in the past.

"Drive safe," she snapped back.

He didn't bother to reply. She was left with a dead phone in her hand and another ache in her chest.

The note was right there, propped against a coffee mug, when she finally got back to her condo a little past two in the morning.

*Maybe we'll pull up at the same intersection again sometime.*

That was it. No *It was great seeing you again*. No *Call me*. Not so much as a hint that they'd reconnected in the most elemental, mutually satisfying way. And it *was* mutual, Swish thought as she crushed the note in an angry fist. He'd wanted her. As much as she'd wanted him.

Still wanted him.

The realization was as unwelcome as it was irritating. They'd tried the happily-ever-after once. It hadn't worked then. It wouldn't work now. Nothing had changed.

The next few weeks kept Swish up to her eyeballs with work. As busy as she was, though, she couldn't seem to regain her usual energy and equilibrium.

The spill containment and recovery efforts proceeded on track. Reps from the EPA and the Arizona Department of Environmental Quality fully endorsed her team's efforts. The booms contained the oil slick on the lake and the skimmers removed the surface contaminants, while the soil vapor extraction system scooped up and vacuumed the contaminated subsoil.

Yet she'd flash on the memory of those few hours in Gabe's arms at the craziest moments. In the middle of a boring staff meeting. Or in her office, while staring sightlessly at some report. More than once she got all mopey, even teary-eyed.

She had to remind herself that she'd lived through separations and a final bust-up before. She'd live through this one, too.

An unexpected visit from Dingo in early June raised her spirits. He was passing through Phoenix on his way to Tuscon. Some kind of business meeting, she gathered, although Dingo tended to be as vague about his life after the military as he'd been while wearing a uniform. They agreed to meet at one of her favorite Mexican restaurants just a few miles from Luke's main gate.

A call from the Staff Judge Advocate working the spill claims delayed Swish, so she got to the restaurant fifteen minutes late. She waved off the hostess with the explanation that she was meeting someone, took a half-dozen steps into the popular eatery and stopped dead.

Good grief! Was that Dingo in a charcoal-gray worsted suit and red power tie? The military cop whose lethal security forces had protected Swish and her team five or six years back, when they'd been ferried into a highly classified location to lay down a runway for the air assault to follow? He'd been Captain Andrews, then. Captain Blake Andrews. His face smeared with camo paint, his weapon at the ready, he'd looked as tough and scary as they came.

He still looked tough. And, yes, a little scary, but so damned handsome. Swish could certainly understand why Chelsea Howard had latched onto him. She was no slouch herself in the looks department. The two of them, Swish mused, made a striking couple.

Returning his wave, she wove her way through the tables. Her sand-colored BDUs caught more than a few glances. They also generated a good number of smiling nods. Americans in general—and the folks in the various communities surrounding Luke AFB, in particular— took pride in their military, which only added to the pride Swish herself took in the uniform she wore. And that led to the question she posed to Dingo when he commented on the ripple her appearance had stirred.

"Do you miss it?" she asked curiously.

"The uniform? Or knowing you're a small part of something big and really important?"

"Either. Both."

"Sometimes. But there are other ways to serve the public."

He didn't mention Gabe. Or the fact that his buddy was now mayor of Small Town, America. He didn't have to. But she was half relieved, half disappointed when he aimed the conversation toward another mutual acquaintance.

"I stopped by to see Cowboy and Alex last week."

Swish accepted the menu the waiter handed her and waved off anything but water. As much as she would've loved an icy margarita, she didn't drink while on duty.

"I haven't talked to either of them since the Bash. How're they doing?"

"Good. Alex's stomach is in the overripe watermelon range now." He paused, gave her an assessing stare. "Cowboy said he'd talked to Gabe."

And there it was.

"Supposedly," Dingo said, "Gabe's deep-sixed his half-formed plan to get married again."

Her reaction was instant and visceral. A brief flicker of sadness for her ex. A surge of guilty relief. And stupid, irrational, completely selfish joy. She wallowed its incandescent glow for several moments before guilt pushed front and center again.

"Did Cowboy say why he called it off?"

"No."

Dingo knew, though. Or guessed. She saw the speculation in the look he leveled at her. To deflect it, she waited until the server took their order, then turned the tables.

"What about you and your oh-so-delectable Vegas showgirl? Last I heard, you and Ms. Chelsea were heading right for hot and heavy."

"We're there. Or we were."

The slow tide of red that darkened his cheeks surprised Swish. In all the years she'd known Blake Andrews, she'd never seen him flustered or fidgety. Until now. He shifted in his seat. Crossed his knee. Uncrossed it again. Returned her gaze with a scowl.

"That woman has me wrapped six ways to Sunday. Every time I think I've got a handle on her, she goes off in a totally different direction. Like the last time I flew into Vegas to see her."

His tone vectored toward petulant. Fascinated, Swish

watched his facial expressions follow the same downward trajectory.

"I bought a ticket for the show at the Wynn. Paid top dollar for a VIP seat, right up front. I was going to surprise her with dinner and...well...whatever afterward."

"From the sound of it, I'm guessing 'whatever' didn't happen."

"The show didn't happen! Or Chelsea's part in it, anyway. Took me three calls and a face-to-face with the production supervisor before I found out she damned near drowned in her last appearance. He fired her. So what does she do?" he demanded fiercely.

"I can't even begin to imagine."

Swish couldn't. She really couldn't. She'd met the flamboyant, long-legged dancer for the first time at this year's Badger Bash, a mere three weeks ago.

Three weeks since she'd driven home in the early dawn. Three weeks since she'd spotted Ole Blue across a deserted intersection. Three weeks since she'd come to the bitter realization that she still loved her husband. *Ex*-husband, dammit. *Ex!*

"She goes to work at Treasure Island, that's what happened!"

"I hear they have a great magic show," she commented, scrambling to catch up.

"They do, except Chelsea's not in it. She's one of the outdoor pirates who swarm the English warship. She swings across the lagoon on a damned rope. Every hour on the hour."

"Not a great gig for a dancer," Swish agreed weakly.

"Ya think?" He leaned forward, his gray eyes shooting ice chips. "The fool woman can't swim."

"So why do they keep hiring her for these aquatic gigs?"

"She's got friends. Lots of friends."

"Well…"

"Well nothing. She's an idiot, as I tried to point out last time we were together."

"Uh-oh."

*Last*, Swish bet, being the operative word. Dingo confirmed that with a frustrated slap of his menu on the colorful tile table.

"Uh-oh is right. She axed me, just like Gabe axed his almost-fiancée."

*And me*, Swish wanted to add. *He axed me, too.* She couldn't put *all* the blame for their last split on him. Still…

"Enough about Chelsea and me," Dingo said, recovering his customary cool. "What's going on with you?"

"Not much, aside from a massive fuel spill, an around-the-clock recovery effort and feeling totally wiped most of the time."

"Wiped? Captain Superwoman? What happened to the inexhaustible energy that made the rest of us groan and beg for relief while you were just getting wound up?"

"Guess I just don't wind as tight as I used to."

He sat back, studying her with the beginning of a frown. "You look a little wiped, too. Still gorgeous, of course, but tired. Maybe you should see a doc."

"Nah." She forced a smile. "It's just the spill. It had me going day and night there for a while. I'll be fine now that we've got a handle on it."

Except she couldn't seem to reclaim her usual levels of energy and enthusiasm. Even Mike Gentry commented on it when he and Swish drove out to check on the removal of the last of the booms the following week. May had melted into a June that was as hot as only Arizona could bake it. The lake surface was diamond-bright, the fumes that had formerly hovered above it gone, thank God.

"Breathing through a respirator would've been torture in this heat," she remarked, leaning a hip against Mike's vehicle.

"It's pretty well torture anytime." The bio-environmental engineer slanted her a quick look. "You okay, Captain? You look tired."

"You're the second person who's told me that." She made a face and tucked a loose strand of hair back into the bun at the nape of her neck. "I'd better start taking vitamins or gulping down some Power Red."

"You might want to have the doc run a few tests," Mike commented. "You may have sucked in some fumes."

She hadn't exhibited any of the classic symptoms, like irritation of the eyes or nose, coughing or blood in her sputum. But she couldn't deny feeling a little out of breath at times. Especially in this heat. And she was too smart to brush off the possibility that she *had* sucked in some toxic fumes. Back at the office, she made an appointment with her primary care manager at the base hospital.

When she walked up to the entrance of 56th Medical Group's sand-colored two-story facility the following morning, the sun burned in another blistering blue sky. The fat, prickly pear cactus that stood sentinel beside the hospital's front door was taking the heat better than Swish was.

"I don't understand it," she told Dr. Bhutti. "I pulled two deployments to Iraq, one to Afghanistan. The heat didn't bother me half as much at either place."

The dark-eyed physician looped her stethoscope around her neck. She and Swish had formed a tight bond at their first meeting, having both served in combat zones.

"Are you hydrating adequately?"

"Forty-eight to sixty-four ounces every day, although lately I seem to be more thirsty than usual."

"Alcohol intake?"

"Minimal. I haven't even felt like a beer after work."

"How much time do you spend in the sun?"

"Three or four hours a day when we have construction or environmental projects underway. Other times, not so much."

"Any chance you could be pregnant? A woman's basal temperature elevates during pregnancy, which makes her more prone to dehydration, heat exhaustion and heat cramps."

"No, I…"

Swish stopped, her breath blocking her throat. An image of Gabe digging a crumpled foil package out of his wallet leaped into her head. How long did he say he'd been carrying the damned thing around? A year? And she'd been so tickled by the fact he hadn't used it with Miss Priss.

"I guess I *could* be."

The doc rolled back her stool. "Well, we'll know soon enough. I'll write an order for a lab test. You may want to cut back on your exposure to the heat until we get the results. And keep drinking plenty of water."

Shock eddied into the first wavelets of panic. "Can't I pee on a stick or something? Find out now?"

"Hang loose. I'll get a kit."

Swish edged off the exam table, her boots thudding on the floor. Too agitated to sit, she paced the tiny room. She couldn't be pregnant. The odds couldn't be *that* stacked against her and Gabe!

A chance meeting at a traffic light. One hot and heavy session between the sheets. Okay, two. Three? No, just two. She'd climaxed first. She was sure she had. Then she'd straddled Gabe's hips and pumped him for all she was worth.

She'd been so eager, so impatient. He hadn't been exactly gentle, either. The condom could've popped anytime during their straining and rocking and thrusting. Ha! Who was she kidding? The roof could've fallen in on them and they wouldn't have noticed.

Dammit all to hell!

She was standing with her arms crossed, boots planted wide, glaring at a chart depicting the pulmonary system, when Dr. Bhutti returned.

"Here's a home pregnancy kit and the lab slips for your blood and urine tests. But be advised that the results from these kits are unofficial as they're not always reliable," she cautioned. "There's a restroom next to the lab. Pee in one of the cups and leave the sample to be analyzed. The home kit is yours to use whenever."

No way Swish was going to wait for the Air Force to do its thing. Clutching the lab slip and the home kit, she threaded her way through a large area crowded with uniformed personnel, retirees and their families, some waiting for prescriptions to be filled, others waiting to called in to see a doc. With almost twenty-six thousand folks eligible for care at the Luke Hospital, it was always a busy place.

She handed the tech at the lab desk the doc's order. "Urine sample first, Captain, then we'll take your blood. You'll find the necessary supplies and instructions in the restroom next door."

It wasn't her first time having to pee in a cup. Every active-duty member had to do a random urinalysis at least once a year. Once every two years for Guard and Reserve members. There were all kinds of safeguards built into the process. An observer had to be present. The donor had to write his or her name on the plastic bottle in the presence of that witness, making it, in essence, a legal document. A rigorous chain-of-custody record was completed by every person at every step of the process. Consequently, Swish had filled her share of little plastic cups. And for at least the tenth or twelfth or twentieth time, she wondered why the hell someone hadn't invented a better way for women to hit the target.

She finally got the cup half full, set it on the edge of the sink and ripped open the home kit. Her palms got clammy as she extracted an eyedropper and a test strip encased in plastic wrap. She closed her eyes for a moment, the dropper gripped between thumb and forefinger. What if the test was positive? What if she was carrying the child Gabe had always wanted? What would she do? What would he do?

They'd work it out, she decided fiercely. One way or another. Jaw set, she suctioned up a small sample of pale gold urine and dropped it on the test strip.

She no idea how long she stood staring at the bright

purple splotch that blossomed on the strip. Long enough for someone to rattle the door handle once, then rattle a few moments later. A third, distinctly impatient shake tore her gaze from the lavender bloom.

"Hey! Anyone in there?"

"I'll be out in a sec."

She collected the home kit elements and stuffed them back in their box, then tossed it in the trash. Capping the urine cup, she used the Sharpie provided by the lab to write her last name on a label, slapped it on the cup and placed the sample on the shelf as instructed. A brief twirl sent the sample into the lab. She emerged and yielded the restroom to a beefy, irritated lieutenant colonel.

"All yours, sir."

Not until she'd rolled up her sleeve and stretched out her arm for the blood test the doc had ordered did the possible ramifications hit her. If she *had* breathed in toxic fumes… If her blood had contained residual gases when the egg fertilized by Gabe's squiggly little sperm had worked its way to her uterus… If those gases had impacted the baby's subsequent cell formation…

"Captain!"

She turned a wild, unseeing stare on the lab tech who'd just stuck a needle in her vein.

"Don't faint on me, Captain! Look up at the ceiling. Breath deep. Slow. There, we're done."

## Chapter Four

When Swish drove to work early the next morning she carried the effects of a long, worried night. Her eyes ached, her skin felt drum tight and her thoughts continually skidded off track. Not even putting the top down on her T-bird and cruising along with the sparse early traffic could blow out the cobwebs. Her stomach stayed knotted until Dr. Bhutti's call at zero-eight-forty.

"Congratulations, Captain. It's official. You're pregnant."

"What about the blood tests?"

"They came back clean. No evidence of any damage to your respiratory system. Your heart and lung functions are normal."

"How about the baby? Could it have been affected by toxic fumes even if nothing showed up in the tests?"

"Unlikely, in my professional opinion, but why don't

we talk about that when you come in to discuss your pregnancy profile. Does this afternoon at sixteen hundred work for you?"

"I'll be there."

Swish hung up, careening wildly between relief and the knowledge her life had just veered off in an unplanned and totally scary direction. Somewhere in the dark reaches of the night she'd eliminated any thought of an abortion. Even with the fear hanging over her like a double-bladed ax that the fetus might've been affected by fumes, she knew she'd see the pregnancy through.

Her mother was a deacon in their church, her dad a retired county assessor. They never talked politics or religion outside the house, but they'd raised their daughter with a very traditional set of values. They'd also been broken-hearted when Swish and Gabe divorced. Aside from losing a son-in-law they both adored, they had to at least temporarily shelve their hope for a brood of noisy, boisterous grandchildren.

They'd be surprised but supportive at the news that Swish was pregnant. In the meantime, she'd have to make major changes in her personal life *and* her career. A pregnancy profile dictated limits on physical training, body weight requirements and environmental exposures. It also disqualified her for worldwide duty and took her off mobility status during her pregnancy and for at least six weeks afterward.

Damn! She'd worked so hard to achieve command of her rapid response engineering team. If the team had to deploy now, it would go without her. Cringing at the thought, Swish went down the hall and rapped on the door of her boss's office.

Lieutenant Colonel Spence Hawthorne had commanded the 56th Civil Engineering Squadron for less than a month. Hawthorne had barely had time to get to know his people—or they him—but what Swish had seen so far impressed her. She had no idea how he'd take the news that the leader of his Prime BEEF team was about to come off mobility status for the next year, though.

He reacted pretty much the way she anticipated, given that he knew she was divorced. Very cautiously. "You're pregnant?"

"That's what the tests say."

"Are, uh, congratulations in order?"

For the first time since Dr. Bhutti suggested she might be pregnant, Swish felt her lips curve in a grin. "Yeah, they are."

"Okay, then." Stretching out a bear-sized paw, he came around from behind his desk and pumped her hand. "Congratulations, Captain. Now, who do you recommend to take over for you as Prime BEEF commander?"

Wham! Just like that she was displaced. Although she'd come in prepared for exactly that question, it still hit hard. "Captain Donaldson's my designated alternate. And Lieutenant Harbaugh would be a good back-fill for him."

"I'll take a look at their records. What's happening with the spill?"

"We're on track with the cleanup. EPA's promised to sign off on it this week."

"Good job, Swish."

"Thanks. There's one more thing."

"I'm listening."

"I'd like to take some leave." She drew in a breath,

let it out. "I need to go home and tell my ex-husband that the weekend we spent together last month has produced some unexpected consequences."

"That should be an interesting conversation."

"No kidding."

"How long do you need?"

"I've racked up so much leave that I'm in use-or-lose status. So I'm thinking two weeks, starting after my prenatal check."

"Go." He approved her request with only one caveat. "Just be sure you come back."

Dr. Bhutti had told her that most initial prenatal appointments weren't scheduled until after the eighth week. Swish was just hitting her seventh, but the doc understood her concerns and got her in with Dr. Evans the following Monday.

The visit was a long one, with more urine and blood samples; checks of blood pressure, height and weight; a pelvic exam and pap smear; and an ultrasound that confirmed a due date based on Swish's encounter with Gabe. The doc took a detailed family and genetic history and went over her deployment record in some detail. He also assured her the blood test would verify the RH factor, hemoglobin and hematocrit, as well as check for hepatitis B, HIV, rubella and syphilis and do another screen for any toxic blood gases.

"Given your concerns, Captain, I suggest we do another, noninvasive blood test at about ten weeks to check for genetic abnormalities like Down syndrome or other chromosomal problems."

Gulping, she agreed.

* * *

With the prenatal visit behind her, Swish debated whether to fly or drive back to Oklahoma. It was only a little over fourteen hours by car. Easily doable in a day.

Or she could break it up with an overnight stop in Albuquerque to visit with Cowboy and his very pregnant wife. Just as Gabe had been planning to do when he'd spotted his ex idling at a red light across an intersection.

The irony wasn't lost on her, but she figured Alex might have some good advice on what to expect in the coming months. More to the point, two easy days on the road would give Swish time to figure out what long-distance parenting arrangements she should propose to Gabe. She didn't doubt for a moment he'd want to be involved in their child's life. They'd just have to work out how much and how often.

A call to Alex that evening resulted in a warm invitation and a rueful explanation. "Ben's not here. He got hit with one of those short notice, I'll-have-to-kill-you-if-I-tell-you-where training exercises. So Maria and I would love some company."

"Great. I should be there by five tomorrow afternoon, if that works for you."

"Works perfectly. See you then."

She left her condo just as dawn was coloring the sky and hit I-10 well before it turned into a one long stop-and-go. The rising sun was in her face this time, instead of the rearview mirror, and the glorious red-and-gold sunrise gave her spirits a decided lift.

Her good mood took a temporary dive when she saw the sign for Exit 134. The same exit she'd pulled off on that fateful morning to hit the ladies' room. As the

McDonald's sign flashed by, she couldn't help thinking how different her life would be right now if she'd crossed her legs and held it. Or, once off the interstate and stopped at the traffic light, if she'd waited for the light to turn green, zipped through the intersection, waved to ex and continued on her merry way.

Right. Like life gave anyone do-overs. Shrugging off the useless shouldda, wouldda, coulddas, she put the exit behind her. Twenty minutes later she turned onto I-17 and headed for the mountains.

She stopped for coffee in New River and lunch in Flagstaff. As always, the majestic San Francisco peaks painted a palette of colors that ranged from hazy green at their base to stone-cold granite near the jagged peaks. Even this late in June she could see a trace of white on the distant Humphrey's Peak.

By the time she'd cruised past Gallup and hit Albuquerque's outskirts, she was ready to take a break. And pee! It was probably purely psychological, but now that she knew she was pregnant the need came even more urgently. Refusing to think about how Gabe would tease her about her bladder battles now, she tracked Mapquest to Alex and Cowboy's address.

Their casita looked like an earth-toned adobe box on the outside but Swish detected an artist's flair in the chilis dangling from raffia ropes and the cactus branching fat arms strung with twinkling white lights and a cloud of colorful, fluttering butterflies.

Alex met her at the door with a hug that she made her angle sideways to accommodate her now bulging belly. Swish battled an instant stab of envy for the mom-to-be's cotton tunic sporting an arch of colorful spangles.

"You look like a giant rainbow."

"I'm certainly a giant something," Alex returned, laughing.

The casita's lush interior was another celebration of Alex's artistic talents. The desert-toned walls, the sofas and chairs covered in green cactus and red chili patterns, the Native American prints and baskets on the walls all delighted Swish. But it was the magnificent Eagle Dancer occupying a place of honor on the mantel above the fireplace that drew her like a magnet. She'd only been assigned to Luke for four months, but she'd spent enough time in and out of other bases in the Southwest to recognize the exquisite workmanship that had produced this carved wooden kachina with its feathers and intricate turquoise beading.

"This is gorgeous!"

"I think so, too."

With a misty smile, Alex rested her arms on the tummy Dingo had described as an overripe watermelon. A slight understatement, Swish decided.

"It was my wedding present to Ben."

Her use of Cowboy's given name was a little jolt. A small but subtle reminder that she was, if not an outsider, at least not lodged at the epicenter of that tight, inner military circle. With her thriving business, Alex maintained a life and an individuality independent of her tangential connection to the military.

Gabe had cut even that tangential connection. He lived a life apart from her and the Air Force now. Was it fair of Swish to pull him back into the periphery of that circle? She was still wrestling with that question.

"Maria's over at her friend Dinah's house," Alex announced as she led the way into the kitchen. "So I made two pitchers of margaritas. High-test for you, virgin for me."

She picked up a frosted green pitcher and was ready to pour when Swish shook her head. "Better make that virgin for both of us."

"Why? You're staying the night, aren't you? Not driving anywhere until... Oh!"

Alex's dark brows shot up, and Swish nodded in response to the unspoken question.

"Yep, me, too."

"Since when?" Plunking the pitcher back onto the tiled counter, she answered her own question. "Wait! You were drinking at the Bash last month so you must've just found out."

"I did."

Alex glanced down the counter, looked up. Swish guessed immediately what was coming. Cowboy's wife was as fiercely loyal to her friends as any of the Badger's protégées were to theirs.

"Chelsea told me Blake Andrews stopped by Phoenix to visit you," Alex said, her voice several degrees cooler than before.

"We met for lunch. Just lunch."

The other woman held her gaze for a moment longer, then nodded. "Good to know."

"But what's with Chelsea's new gig at Treasure Island? Dingo says she swings across the lagoon on a rope every hour on the hour."

Her loyalty to her former roommate satisfied, Alex laughed. "Not anymore. All it took was one dunk. She's unemployed again."

Not for long, Swish bet. If those mile-long legs and generous boobs didn't wow some other producer, the dancer's infectious laugh and sparkling personality would. Wishing Dingo the best of luck with his on-again, off-again girlfriend, she turned to more immediate concerns.

"This whole pregnancy bit is so new, I haven't wrapped my head around it yet. You mind if I pick your brain about what to expect?"

"Pick away!" Alexis poured two virgin drinks, waved Swish to a counter stool and plopped onto the one next to her. "Where do you want to start? The bloating? The gas? The swollen ankles or the fact that one whiff of sizzling fajitas makes me puke?"

"Actually, I was hoping you'd clue me in to some of the legal ramifications. I know you and Cowboy adopted Maria over her natural father's objections. I'll have to work out a custody arrangement, too."

"Ummm, I can see that might be an issue since you and the father aren't married."

"Actually, we were. Once."

"Gabe?" Alex tried her damnedest to choke back her surprise. She didn't quite get there. "Are you telling me Gabe's the father?"

"Yep."

"Where? How?"

"He was driving east on I-10. I was driving west, back to the base."

"You mean the day after the Bash? When he was going to stop by to see us?"

"Yep," Swish said again. "We hooked up by chance, then went our separate ways."

"So that's why he was so late getting here! Wait till I tell Ben." Her eyes danced. "Are you two planning to get back together?"

"No. Well. Maybe. At least, as far as it involves the baby." Her shoulders slumping, Swish admitted the truth. "Oh, God, Alex, I don't know *what* we're going to do. I haven't even told Gabe I'm pregnant yet. That's why I took leave and am heading back to Oklahoma."

"Well…" Her hostess used the excuse of topping off their drinks to gather her thoughts. "There are several single moms and military couples in Ben's squadron. I know they have to sign some kind of document detailing who'll take care of their kids if they get deployed."

"I know. A Family Care Plan."

Air Force regulations required that all single parents and military couples with children name a non-military Short-Term Care Provider who could assume care of their child in the event the parent or parents were deployed on short notice. They also had to designate a Long-Term Care Provider willing to assume full responsibility for the child if the parent or parents were deployed for an extended period of time, selected for an unaccompanied overseas tour or assigned to a ship at sea.

Swish didn't doubt for a minute that Gabe would agree to be their child's designated care provider. Assuming, that is, he didn't push for full custody. The possibility had been buzzing around in the back of her mind for most of the day's drive.

"Our situation probably isn't all that unique but it will require some negotiation."

"How so?"

"We got a quickie, no-contest divorce. We'll have to go back to court to address legal custody of our baby."

She'd done some research. The Service Member's Relief Act protected military personnel from having to defend themselves from civil suits—including divorces and child custody hearings—while overseas and not able to defend themselves. The Uniform Deployed Parents Custody and Visitation Act passed in 2012 was a more comprehensive attempt to balance the rights of service members, the other parent and the best interests of the child involved. Her situation with Gabe fell somewhere in the middle of all that legalese.

"I'm sorry, Suze. I wish I could help. Our petition to adopt Maria sprang from a completely different set of legal circumstances. I can refer you to a really good family practice attorney, though. He's licensed here in New Mexico, which wouldn't help if you have to petition an Arizona court, but he's one of the best in the field."

"Thanks. Hopefully Gabe and I can work all this out amicably. If not, I may take you up on that referral."

"Good enough. Now let's talk maternity tops. I'm developing a whole new line of tanks and tees celebrating big bellies."

"If they're all as gorgeous as that rainbow you're wearing, I'll take one of each."

"No way. You, my friend, will get a one-of-a-kind Alexis Scott design."

The lively, bright-eyed Maria and her black-and-white cat entertained Swish at breakfast the next morning while Alex darted over to her workshop. She returned just as her guest was getting ready to leave and presented her with a stretchy, cap-sleeved royal-blue top that featured the Air Force insignia in sparkling silver and darker blue crystals. Above them, Alex had emblazoned Warrior Mom in bright, bold red.

"Best I could do on short notice. Try it on and see if it fits."

Swish ducked into the powder room off the hall and exchanged her sun-faded 56th Fighter Wing T-shirt for glittering blue and red crystals.

"This is fantastic, Alex. Thank you!"

The designer tapped a finger against her chin. "It'll do for a rush job. But I'm working on more elaborate designs for each of the four military services. I should have the prototypes ready when you come back through. You'll have to give me your honest opinion."

"Will do," Swish promised.

With the morning sun once again in her face, Swish hit I-40 and headed east through Tijeras Pass. Even in high summer, wind whistled through the narrow pass with enough gusto to rock the car. Once through the canyon, the Sandia Mountains fell behind her and the landscape flattened to high desert plateaus scarred by zigzagging washes. Triple-strand barbed wire defined widely scattered ranches. Angled snow fences were positioned to keep the interstate clear come winter.

She stopped to pee twice that morning. Once in Tucumcari. Again just over the Texas state line. Lunch was chicken and dumplings at the Cracker Barrel in Amarillo. She made another pit stop when she hit the Oklahoma state line. Fifty miles later, the rugged mesas of the Panhandle gave way to rolling plains that tugged at something deep inside her. This was the land that had nourished her. Nourished Gabe. Their baby's roots went deep into the red Oklahoma soil.

She exited I-40 some thirty miles outside Oklahoma City and had to smile at the oversize water tower proclaiming Yukon as the birthplace of Garth Brooks. Gabe had saved his earnings as a pizza delivery boy for months to buy tickets for Brooks's big concert at the Chesapeake Center in Ok-City the week Swish turned eighteen. She still had every song the country star had ever recorded in her iTunes library.

Once through Yukon, she followed a spear-straight county road nine miles south to the town of Cedar Creek. Born and bred in this sleepy, tree-shaded town, she knew its history backward and forward. Not surprising, since she'd worked one entire summer at the town's musty records office and history center.

From prehistoric times, hunter-gatherers had camped alongside the creek lined with stunted, twisty-limbed cedars. The same creek she and Gabe used to swim in. And go skinny-dipping in. And…

Biting down on her lower lip, she blanked the memory of those hours splashing in the sun-dappled creek and let her gaze roam over broad, flat fields. The area's primary industry had always been agriculture. Early settlers had planted huge orchards and plowed acre after acre of rich soil. Swish and almost every other kid she knew had earned spending money picking asparagus, carrots and strawberries in the spring, cantaloupe and watermelon and sweet corn in the summer, apples and pears in the fall.

Which was how Gabe had busted three ribs, she remembered with a wry smile. He'd had to show off. Demonstrate to her and his pals what a fast picker he was by reaching too far out on a limb. His subsequent tumble off his ladder had scared the dickens out of Swish. It had also made him miss most of his junior

year football season and almost cost him his scholarship to OU.

And that, she acknowledged grimly as she forced
yet another vivid scene out of her head, was why she'd
made such infrequent visits to her parents in the past
few years. Every street, every dusty storefront, even the
elementary school, held too many memories.

Fighting those memories, she eased off the gas and
made a slow drag down Main. The changes were all too
noticeable. A depressing number of antique and second-
hand shops had moved in when the original businesses
relocated to properties closer to the Walmart on the east
side of town. The local bank that had passed out lolli-
pops to every kid who came in with their parents was
gone, replaced by a drive-through chain branch.

To her delight, though, Ruby's Cafe still occupied a
prime spot at the corner of Main and 3rd Street. And a
hand-printed placard said the bandstand at the center
of Veterans' Memorial Park still hosted summer Sat-
urday evening concerts.

She noticed even more changes when she turned off
Main onto the street that followed twisty, turning Cedar
Creek. Yards that had been dappled with weeds when
she'd last visited her folks were neatly mowed, their
edges trimmed. Homes that had looked a little run-
down had new coats of paint. Even the junker on the
corner of Cedar and 5th had undergone an amazing
metamorphosis. The awful clutter on its front porch
had disappeared. So had the three rusty vehicles that
used to roost on cinderblocks in its drive.

She spotted a surprising number of new homes, too.
Classy brick-and-river-stone facades. High-pitched

roofs. Two- and three-car garages. All set on a bend of the creek previously occupied by an abandoned mill.

That had to be Gabe's doing. All of this! As she knew all too well, her ex-husband had an extremely low tolerance for clutter. His years in the military had only exacerbated his type A personality. From all appearances, it looked as though Cedar Creek's determined young mayor had demolished the crumbling mill and opened all those pretty lots with their sloping views of the creek to a new wave of settlers. She guessed they probably were probably spillover from the sprawling, ever-expanding Federation Aviation Administration's training center less than fifteen miles away. Looking at the manicured lawns and elegant facades, she'd bet her next paycheck that Gabe intended to turn their once sleepy farm town into one of OKC's more desirable bedroom communities.

She would've won her bet, as her parents confirmed a mere half hour after they'd joyously welcomed their only chick back to her childhood home. He dad was older and grayer but still trim and energetic. Her spritely, gregarious mother now sported glowing turquoise tips at the ends of her silvery bob.

Swish's open-mouthed astonishment at the bright color delighted her mom. Almost as much as when they took up their favorite positions on the front porch and her daughter bit into a raisin-pecan-oatmeal cookie with an ecstatic sigh.

"Iced tea. Fresh-baked cookies. I'm home."

As easily, as naturally as that, she slipped back into her Cedar Creek skin. She was a daughter, a neighbor, a friend to so many who still lived here. Luke AFB, the fuel spill, her Prime BEEF Team all belonged to another world, another person. As they had so many times, she and her mom shared the porch swing. Her dad sat in the ratty, high-backed wicker fan chair that Mary Elizabeth Kingfisher Jackson had been threatening to get rid of for the past ten years.

"What's with all these new houses?" Swish asked. "Where's everyone coming from?"

"I don't know," her number-cruncher dad said. "And I don't care. You wouldn't believe it, Suze. With all the newcomers, we could ask two or even three times what we would've asked a few years ago for this property."

She planted a foot on the floor and stopped the swing's gentle motion. "Are you guys thinking of selling?"

"Probably not for a few years yet. But we're feeling our age more with each passing day. If the value of the house keeps rising due to Gabe's clever outreach pro—ow!"

Wincing, he yanked his ankle out reach of his wife's sharp-pointed mule. He couldn't miss her warning scowl, however. "Sorry, Suzanne. When you called to tell us you were coming home, your mom made me swear I wouldn't mention Gabe."

"It's okay." She took a sip and let the sugary-sweet tea give her courage. "As a matter of fact, Gabe and I sort of…uh…reconnected last month."

Hope sprang into her parents' eyes. So obvious. So painful that she almost blurted out that she was pregnant. She couldn't, though. Not until she'd told Gabe.

"Whooo-wheee!" Hooting, her dad slapped his thigh. "Are you two are getting back together?"

"Oh, baby!" Her eyes filming with tears, Mary shot an arm around her daughter's shoulders and hugged her joyfully. "You don't know how long and hard we've prayed for this. You and Gabe belong together. You always have."

Acutely uncomfortable, she explained as gently as she could. "We're not *back* together, Mom. We just spent a few hours together last month."

"But you came home. All the way from Arizona just to see him again. Those hours had to mean something."

Oh, they did! Much more than she could share at this particular moment. She dodged their hopes with a bright smile.

"I came home to see you *and* Gabe. Right now, though, I'm more interested in our chances of getting dad to fire up that new grill I saw on the back patio without singeing his eyebrows off."

The oblique reference to a long-ago family camping trip had her mom laughing and her dad huffing indignantly.

Hours later she drifted toward an exhausted slumber in her old bedroom. The same daisy-splashed comforter draped her bed. The same ancient iMac sat on her desk. And the same posters decorated the walls.

God, how she'd crushed on Linkin Park. Looking back, she realized the rock band had showcased her induction into the bewildering mysteries of adolescence. Menstruation. Weird sensations low in her belly every time Gabe walked her home from school. The startled glance he aimed at her chest that hot spring day they skipped World History to skinny-dip in Cedar Creek.

*Whoa!* She could still see his surprise. Still hear the indignation. *When the hell did you get boobs, Susie Q?*

The past swamped her, and she gave up thinking of

herself as Swish. To everyone here, she was *Suzanne*, the obnoxiously inquisitive kid who'd delved into those dusty archives at the Cedar Creek records office. *Suze*, the baton-twirling majorette who'd pranced ten paces ahead of her high school band in every hometown parade and state competition. *Susie Q*, the eager bride who'd married the only man she'd ever loved.

And *USAF Lieutenant Suzanne Hall*, she tacked on with a small pang. So thrilled with her construction engineering degree from OU. So eager to raise her hand and be sworn in as a second lieutenant. So freakin' proud of her shiny gold bars. And so damned eager to shake off Oklahoma's red dust.

Scrunching her eyes shut, she blocked the colorful reminders of her past that surrounded her. She might be stretched out in the same bed she'd dreamed in for so many years, but she was *not* the same hopelessly idealistic teen who'd believed in happily-ever-after. She'd come home for one reason and one reason only.

She would call Gabe first thing in the morning and arrange a meeting. She'd have to give him time to get over the shock. God knew she was still dealing with it. Once he'd recovered, they would calmly, rationally work out a child custody agreement. One that recognized the rights and desires of both parents. Then they'd go their separate ways.

Again.

Fighting a stupid rush of tears, Suze dragged the sheet up over her head.

## *Chapter Five*

Suzanne Jackson Hall was back in town.

Gabe heard about it when he dropped into Ruby's for the Thursday evening meatloaf special. Three different people couldn't wait to let him know they'd spotted his ex-wife cruising Main in a berry-red T-bird earlier that afternoon.

He got another confirmation of the news when he stopped to fill up Ole Blue up at Jerry Dixon's Gas 'N' Go on his way home. While Jerry ran his credit card, he oh-so-casually let it drop that when his wife, Janice, had gone out to water her hydrangeas, she'd waved to Suze and her folks from across the street.

So Gabe wasn't surprised when his mother and two of his three sisters called that evening to report additional sightings. None of them could cite the reason for the visit, however, although Gabe suspected someone would nose it out before much longer.

To his surprise, he even heard from Alicia Johnson. The petite, perpetually upbeat Realtor had handled their breakup surprisingly well. She admitted that she'd pretty much given up on him deciding to take their relationship to the next level. But she'd also let him know she was still available if he changed his mind. For a while, anyway.

Actually, her easy acceptance of the split had dinged Gabe's pride a little. At least until he heard through the grapevine that Alicia had attended some black-tie charity function in Oklahoma City on the arm of oil-and-gas magnate Dave Forrester while Gabe was out in California.

Tonight's call, she informed him, sprang from the fact that she still cared about him. Enough to want to be sure he'd heard about his ex. "I know how small towns are," she said with one of her rippling laughs. "You've probably already received a half-dozen reports that Suze is home. But just in case…?"

"I got the word."

"Okay, then." A pause. "Tell her hello from me when you see her."

Yeah, sure. Like *that* was gonna happen.

Gabe never claimed to be the sharpest pencil in the box, especially when it came to understanding the female psyche. Growing up with three sisters had hammered home the unshakable conviction that men and women really did inhabit different emotional planets.

But even he understood why Suze and Alicia had never developed a shred of rapport. A sixth grade Sadie Hawkins dance shortly after Alicia and her folks had moved to Cedar Creek had ignited the initial feud with Gabe caught squarely in the middle.

Then there was the infamous band-room incident in junior high. No one, Gabe included, knew who said what to whom. Neither of the principals involved would discuss it. But Suze quit band and never went back. In his heart of hearts, Gabe suspected the dustup might've had something to do with the fact that she was tone deaf and couldn't play the trumpet worth squat. Even her mother had gently suggested she wasn't a good fit for the church's youth orchestra. Thankfully, Gabe had managed to avoid getting caught in the middle of that one.

"It's too bad Suze and I ended up rivals," Alicia admitted. "I would've liked to be her friend. She's so darn smart and a natural-born leader. Not to mention the fact that she had the hottest stud in three counties dangling at the end of her line."

Gabe returned the only safe answer he could come up with. "I'll tell her you said hey."

Then he waited. All the rest of that evening and a good chunk of the next morning.

With school out for the summer, he didn't have classes to prepare for. No searching for new ways to pound the relevance of history into high schoolers whose hormones had taken possession of their brains. Even the tennis clinics had been put on hold in this 100-plus degree heat. Nor did he have a city council meeting to stretch his patience and diplomatic skills to the breaking point. So, right up until nine-forty-five on that hot, steamy June morning, it was just him and Doofus.

"What do you think?" he asked the chocolate-eyed, lop-eared mutt. "Is she gonna call or not?"

The hound lifted his head from his outstretched

paws. Angled his head. Then huffed out a distinctly dog-flavored breath, his dewlaps quivering in ecstasy as Gabe scratched behind his ears.

"You're a big help," Gabe chided with a wry smile. He still hadn't figured out how he'd come to share his life with this oversize mutt with a wiry, corkscrew coat, the instincts of a hunter and the personality of an over-eager puppy.

Gabe had found him shivering under Ole Blue, every rib plainly visible and his coat a tangled mess. He'd brought the dog in for the night, intending to take him to the shelter if no one responded to the notices he put out. That was last November. Seven months later they were still housemates.

The size of a small horse, the dog ate like there was no tomorrow and went nuts at the sound of a bell or buzzer. *Any* bell or buzzer. The phone. The front door. The microwave. The washer dinging the end of a cycle. So when Suze finally called, Doofus reacted with typical hysteria.

Gabe was in his beat-up leather armchair, feet propped on the hassock, reviewing Cedar Creek's revised five-year budget on his laptop while the dog sprawled, paws in the air, on the floor beside him. Jerked from his sleep, the hound leaped up and raced for the front door, woofing his fool head off and demonstrating yet again how he'd earned his name.

"It's the phone," Gabe shouted over his ear-shattering barks. "Hey! Doofus! It's the phone! Oh, for...! Hang on a sec, Suze."

He pushed out of the chair and made for the front door. As soon as it opened, the hound leaped out, ready to take on any and all hostiles. Thoroughly disappointed to find not even a squirrel to chase, Doofus barked out a loud warning just for the heck of it before wheeling back inside. His claws clicked on the hall tiles as he pranced back to the den and plopped down beside Gabe's chair.

"What in the world was that?" Suze wanted to know when Gabe got back on the phone.

"My self-appointed greeting committee. Any sudden noise sends him to the front door in a frenzy of excitement."

"When did you acquire a greeter?"

"About six months back."

She hesitated, then plunged in. "I'm assuming the jungle drums have already telegraphed the news."

"That my ex drove into town yesterday afternoon? Yeah, they have. You took your time getting around to telling me yourself."

He tried, honestly tried, to keep the bite out of his voice. Probably would've done a better job of it if he hadn't lain awake half the damned night wondering why she'd come home so suddenly.

Gabe kept in touch with her folks. He never thought of them as his *ex*-in-laws. Last time they talked a few days ago, both Mary and Ed Jackson were doing well, and Gabe would've heard immediately if they'd suffered some kind of emergency since then. So, if it wasn't her folks who bought her home, it had to be him. Him and their unexpected, unresolved last meeting.

The fierce hope that thought stirred scared the crap out of him. Their separation and divorce had left a mile-wide crater in his heart but he'd recovered. Slowly, painfully, he'd forced himself to adjust to LSS. Life sans Suze.

Hooking up with her last month had ripped the wound open again. For those few, wild hours that he'd cradled her in his arms, Gabe had actually let himself think they could erase the mistakes and hurts of the past and start over. Then she'd leaped out of bed and yanked on her uniform and hadn't bothered to call until seven hours later, when he was already on the road.

He understood she loved her job. He also understood that she was good at it. So freakin' good she'd probably end up as the three-star commander of some joint task force or another.

He also understood about emergency responses. Hell, even here in sleepy Cedar Creek, he and his first responders dealt with their share of disasters. The damage was generally small scale—a vehicle accident or kitchen fire or a tragic drowning—but the impact on people's lives was immediate and too often devastating.

If Gabe hadn't learned anything in the past, tumultuous few years, it was that life didn't hand out any do-overs. No starting from scratch again. Not for him, for Suze, for his constituents or his former targets. Yet damned if his pulse didn't do a quick roll when she requested a face-to-face.

"I need to talk to you. Can we get together for coffee?"

"Sure."

She waited for more, but he refused to make it easy for her.

"Mom said you bought the old Schumann place. That you've been fixing it up. Should I come there?"

"That works."

"Now?"

He was just irritated enough at her for taking so long to call—and at himself for being so anxious to hear the sound of her voice—that he enjoyed the snap in her reply.

"Okay. I'll brew up a fresh pot."

* * *

Suze used the short drive to rein in her temper. She knew exactly why Gabe had pushed her buttons. She would've been pissed, too, if she'd been waiting for her ex to explain why he'd suddenly dropped into town. Assuming, of course, he'd been waiting and not doing the dirty with Miss Priss.

Thank God Dingo had told her Gabe had called it off with Alicia. The relief that Prissy Missy wouldn't become stepmother to the child Suze now carried occupied her thoughts all the way to the Schumann place.

It was one of the older homesteads, set in a curve of the creek, with a natural windbreak provided by a stand of ancient pecan trees that had no doubt yielded their succulent harvest to the hunter-gatherers who'd roamed this area for thousands of years. The first Schumanns to settle in Cedar Creek claimed this choice plat during the land run and put up a wood-framed, two-story house. One of their grandkids—great-grandkids?—had added an L-shaped addition. Another had slapped on some puke-green aluminum siding and lived there until he and his wife passed away. *Their* kids had put the house on the market immediately but it had sat vacant for as long as Suze could remember.

As she turned onto 8th Street, memories of the Schumann place crowded in. How many times had she and Gabe and their pals ignored the *No Trespassing* sign to swim in the shady creek behind the deserted homestead? How many bright September afternoons had they waded through knee-high weeds to reach the pecan orchard and fill gunny sacks with ripe nuts? They'd picked most of the harvest off the ground, although Gabe often attached a hook to a long broom handle so he could reach the lower branches and shake down a golden-brown rain. She could almost taste the luscious chocolate-pecan pies Gabe's mom baked from their harvest.

She would swing by to visit her former mother-in-law in the next day or two. Gabe's sisters, too. Once she and Gabe had worked out a plan for how...

Good God!

Her foot hit the brake. She jerked the convertible to a stop midblock, staring in stunned surprise at what used to be a decrepit, empty shell. The sea of prickly weeds that had surrounded it was gone, replaced by a sweep of tree-shaded lawn and a curving drive. The wraparound porch, once sagging and all but invisible behind a screen of scraggly, overgrown bushes, now sported new railings and support beams painted a clean, inviting white. The nauseating green siding was gone, too. Suze almost didn't recognize the old homestead with those wide windows, river-rock trim and double-wide front door.

And the crepe myrtles. Dear Lord, the crepe myrtles! That huge Dynamite Red at the corner of the porch had been so clogged with strangler vines it had never put out more than a few blooms. And the hedge of Twilight Lavenders alongside the detached garage... She ached to bury her face in those fragrant blossoms and breathe in the scent she always associated with home.

Still marveling at the old homestead's transformation, she took her foot off the brake and turned into the drive. The front door opened just as she glided to a stop. Gabe came out onto the porch, a coffee mug in one hand and the other gripping the collar of a shaggy hound.

The self-appointed greeter boomed a welcome while

his ragged tail sliced the air a mile a minute. Bright-eyed and eager, the dog strained against the hold on his collar until Gabe issued a sharp command. "Sit!"

He obeyed, but his butt continued to wiggle furiously on the varnished porch planking. Suze approached the dog cautiously and held out her hand for him to sniff. After one perfunctory whiff, he drenched her palm with eager, slobbering kisses. Smiling down at his liquid brown eyes and goofy grin, she fell instantly in love.

"Looks like he's part Lab," she commented.

"He is. But the vet thinks he's mostly wire-haired pointing griffon."

"What the heck is a wirehaired pointing whatever?"

"A sporting breed supposedly developed toward the end of the nineteenth century to flush, point and retrieve water fowl and game birds. God knows, he spends more time in the creek than out of it."

"Never heard of a griffon."

"Me, either, until Doofus barreled into my life. He's pretty good at not jumping on folks but when I release him, better be prepared."

Suze dutifully planted both feet and let the hound dance around her a few times. He certainly looked like he wanted to jump up and lick her chin. She could see the eagerness in his quivering, shivering excitement. But he confined his attention to the hand she kept extended until the flick of a bushy tail across the lawn snagged his attention. He whirled, locked on his prey, then took off, barking ferociously at the squirrel who dared invade his domain.

"That'll keep him occupied for a while," Gabe said drily. "C'mon in."

He held the door for her, and Suze took the few steps

onto the porch and into the air-conditioned cool of an entry hall paneled in whitewashed wood.

"There's a powder room," Gabe said with a nod at a nearby door, "if you want to wash off the dog slobber."

"Thanks." She glanced around in genuine appreciation. The interior's transformation was as startling as the exterior's. "I can't believe what you've done with this place. It was still an abandoned wreck last time I was home."

"Fixing it up kept me busy. And," he added on a flat note, "it helped me get my life back on track. I needed something other than teaching and city council meetings to fill my evenings and weekends."

Riiight. That put her squarely in her place.

"I'll wait for you in the kitchen. Straight back and to the left."

Suze took her time in the powder room, her nervousness returning. She used the natural light streaming through the row of glass blocks set above the door to freshen her lip gloss and rake a hand through her hair. She'd worn it down today, with only the sides clipped back to keep it out of her eyes. *Not* because Gabe always liked it that way. And she hadn't chosen her slim white jeans and clingy red tank with him in mind, even if they did mirror their high school colors of cream and firehouse red.

"Okay," she instructed her image in the mirror. "Go do this."

It wasn't hard to find the kitchen, considering that Gabe had knocked out most of the walls on the ground floor. The short entry hall led to a sweeping, sunlit open space that flowed from great room to dining area to kitchen. The great room was all male—oversize leather sofa and chairs, giant flat-screen TV, a walk-around bar in one corner. The dining area boasted a gray plank table and eight upholstered chairs with a centerpiece that stopped Suze in her tracks.

They'd found that gnarly piece of driftwood on their honeymoon! It had washed up on the beach at Galveston and Suze had insisted on lugging it home. She'd always intended to do something with it. Someday.

"I was helping your folks clean out their basement," Gabe explained with a shrug. "They asked if I wanted it."

Her breath hitching, she smoothed a finger over the undulating curves and admired the clever silver candle-holders drilled into the wood at various points. "This is gorgeous. Who did it?"

"An artist friend of Alicia's."

Suze's hand dropped to her side. She kept her expression blank. She was sure she had. But Gabe could read her like an old, dog-eared book.

"It's over between Alicia and me," he said evenly, his hips propped against the butcher block island that ran almost the entire length of his open, airy kitchen. "We shifted our friendship back into neutral when I got home last month."

She had to bite down on the joy that leaped through her. It was too fierce and hot and primitive to think about at the moment. It was also extremely shallow. As much as she disliked Alicia, she had no right to take such selfish delight in a breakup that must have been difficult for Gabe.

"I'm sorry if our interlude in Phoenix messed things up for you."

"No, you're not. Do you want some coffee? Then you can tell me what this unexpected visit is all about."

Oooo-kay. This was how he'd played it on the phone earlier. Short. Abrupt. Not yielding an inch. She couldn't really blame him. She would've been pissed if he'd breezed back into *her* life without warning or explanation.

"Coffee would be good."

While he filled a mug and topped off his own, she moved to stand at the French doors that gave access to a covered flagstone patio. Beyond the patio was another slope of lush lawn. Beyond that was the tree-lined creek.

Doofus was still chasing squirrels, she saw, as the hound streaked across the backyard in full hunt mode. His prey made it to the pecan orchard and darted up a tree, only to perch on a lower limb and jeer at its wildly leaping pursuer.

"Remember how you used to knock ripe pecans down from those branches?" she asked as Gabe passed her a mug.

"I do."

"Does your mom still bake those sinful chocolate-pecan pies?"

"She doesn't bake much of anything anymore. She's had a hard time since the hip replacement."

"I plan to stop by and see her." She raised her gaze to his face. "If it's okay with you?"

The question ignited a spark of anger. "Hell, Suze. You're as much a daughter to her as any of my sisters. You don't need my permission to visit her, any more than I needed yours to help your folks clean out their basement."

"Hey, back off! I was just trying to be polite."

"Screw polite. Why are you here, Suzanne? What's going on?"

"All right! Okay!" She puffed her cheeks and blew out a long breath. "Brace yourself, Mr. Mayor. Your life's about to get knocked off track again."

His brows snapped together. He didn't say anything, though. Just waited with that tight, unreadable expression for her to drop another bomb, like the one that had ended their marriage.

Suze had to do it quick, before she lost her nerve. "I'm pregnant."

His expression didn't change. He didn't so much as blink.

Dying a little inside, she realized she'd been stupid to imagine he'd greet the news with at least a semblance of delight. He'd been so ready to put down roots, so ready to begin their family, but her unwillingness to even negotiate a start date for his dreams had started them down the painful path to divorce. That, and their frequent separations. And her reluctance to put her career on hold. And the brief affair she'd had during their final separation.

Given all those factors, Gabe had to be asking himself some very ugly questions. Like who the father was. And how far along his ex-wife was. And what the hell she intended to do about the pregnancy.

Suze waited for him to unload but he still hadn't broken his silence when Doofus loped up to the French doors and let loose with a roof-rattling woof. Gabe smothered an oath, twisted the door handle and kneed the overjoyed dog aside.

"Cool it, mutt."

Taking Suze's elbow in a fierce hold, he steered her toward the kitchen counter. Eyes smoldering, he thunked down his mug, plucked hers out of her hand and stabbed a finger at one of the high-backed stools. "Sit."

"Gabe, I…"

"No!" He cut her off with a fiery glare. "Me first."

Okay, she deserved this. After all the heartache, all the talk of a baby, she owed it to him to sit and listen while he spilled his anger. So she damned near toppled backward off the stool when he shoved a hand under her hair, gripped her nape in a hard vise and held her steady while he plundered her mouth.

The kiss combined the kick of dark, rich Colombian coffee and unbridled male exuberance. She could taste both, feel both, and responded in kind. Her arms whipped around his neck. Her mouth molded to his.

This was Gabe. Her Gabe.

An achingly familiar joy flooded her heart. It was followed almost instantly by an entirely new sensation. One wrapped in a hundred different shades of happy.

This was Gabe. The father of her child.

Tears burned behind her closed eyelids. She tried to blink them back, but when he broke the kiss and spotted then leaking from the corners of her eyes, he muttered a low curse.

"Hell, Suze. I'm sorry. So damned sorry."

Her lids fluttered up, and she blinked a question from tear-blurred eyes.

"That condom must've been a year old," he said in disgust. "We shouldn't have trusted it. *I* shouldn't have trusted it."

The gruff apology spurred a quick, almost hysterical laugh. "Funny, I was thinking pretty much the same thing for most of that drive from Phoenix to Cedar Creek."

He kept his palm around her nape, his gaze gentle on hers. "That must've been one helluva long drive."

"I broke it up with an overnight in Albuquerque. I wanted to talk to Cowboy's wife, Alex."

"Because she's pregnant, too?" His mouth curved. "You could've waited and talked to any one of my sisters. Between them, they've racked up at least ten years of big bellies, aching backs and room-clearing farts."

Laughing, Suze eased out of his hold. Trust Gabe to tease her through this weepy hormonal moment. "Actually, I wanted to talk to Alex about the custodial agreements. She couldn't offer much help, though, except to suggest we consult a good family practice attorney."

Gabe withdrew, slowly, almost imperceptibly. Suze sensed the wall that came down between them even before he tilted his chin and narrowed those gold-flecked hazel eyes.

"Custodial agreements, huh? As in, how many weeks a year I'm allowed to spend with my child?"

She should've been grateful for his unquestioned acceptance of the fact that the baby was his. Would have, if his tone hadn't alerted her to rocky shoals ahead.

"As in," she replied with deliberate calm, "whether you'll assume full legal responsibility for *our* child if I'm deployed or assigned to a remote locale."

He backed away. Leaned against the island again. Crossed his arms. "So you intend to stay in uniform?"

"That's the plan right now."

"I see." His eyes went as hard as the agates they used to dig out of the creek bank. "Guess we'd better make an appointment with Shirley Stockton."

"Who?"

"She and her husband moved into town from LA

a few years back. He's a supervisor at FAA. She's a lawyer. We don't get all that many child custody cases here in Cedar Creek, but those we do, Shirley usually handles."

Miserable, Suze understood all too well why the air between them had gone from sizzling to frigid in a few short sentences. For a few, unthinking moments, Gabe had equated her pregnancy with a complete change in direction for both of them. He'd assumed the baby would heal the breach of the past three years. That Suze would separate from the Air Force. That the two of them would pick up where they'd left off, and their separate, complicated lives would once again merge.

She'd wanted that, too. For that same, unthinking moment when his mouth covered hers. God, how she'd wanted that!

"We probably should also talk specifics," Gabe said, interrupting her chaotic thoughts. "Like when you're due and how we're going to break the news to our families."

She grimaced. "My folks already jumped on the fact that we hooked up in Phoenix last month. They keep hoping we'll get back together."

"Yeah, well, doesn't sound as though you've considered that as an option."

The cold, dismissive comment brought her off the stool.

"The hell I haven't!" Tears stung her eyes again, and she cursed her out-of-whack hormones. "You think the divorce has been any easier on me than it has on you? I've ached for you, you idiot. I've missed your laugh, your homemade chili, your stupid jokes."

She flung up both hands, palms out and stopped him as he surged toward her.

"I have *not* missed the arguments. Or feeling guilty

about the hours I have to put into my job. Or the pressure you laid on me to separate from the service and spend the rest of my life here in Hicksville, Oklahoma."

She winced, instantly regretting her outburst. "Okay, I didn't mean that last part."

Gabe slumped against the counter again, his face tight and angry. "Oh, yeah, Susie Q, you did. You couldn't wait to shake loose of Cedar Creek."

"And you couldn't wait to get back."

He broke the silence that followed with a curt, "So here we are."

"Here we are," she echoed.

As if sensing the resentment and unhappiness hanging as thick as a cloud in the kitchen, Doofus crowded against Gabe until he dropped a hand and scratched behind a wiry, tufted ear. Eyes closed, the hound succumbed to quivering ecstasy.

"Okay, look. I need a little time to assimilate the fact I'm going to be a father. Why don't we have dinner at Ruby's tonight? Five thirty? We can talk it through then."

"Neutral ground? That works for me. Especially since this is sour cream chicken enchilada night."

Oh, God! She'd dreaded this part but knew if she didn't tell him now, she might not find the courage to do it later.

"While you're assimilating this business of being a father, there's one other bit of information you need to factor in. The day we got together in Phoenix... When I responded to that fuel spill..."

"Yeah?"

"My guys and I were on respirators the whole time we worked the spill."

"But?" he asked, suddenly wary.

"But I felt so tired and draggy for weeks afterward, I was afraid I might have breathed in some toxic fumes."

He stiffened and she rushed on. "The doc ran all kinds of tests. She found no evidence of toxic infiltration in my blood or lungs. None!"

"Did she know you were pregnant?"

"*I* didn't even know! She's the one who told me. She also said she's a hundred percent confident the baby's okay but I thought should... I felt I'd better..." She lifted a hand, let it drop. "I thought you should know."

When he didn't respond, she beat a hasty retreat.

"I'll see you at Ruby's."

## Chapter Six

"Doofus! Let's go!"

Gabe needed to run. Hard. Fast. Slamming the dirt with everything in him.

He'd run track in junior high. Been pretty damned good at it, too. Took home All State honors at both 800 and 1500 meters. In high school, his speed made him a local star on the football field and won him a scholarship to OU. He hadn't racked up as many TDs in college as he had in high school, but he'd more than justified his scholarship.

He'd fallen off his competitive pace in the years since, of course, but could pound some serious pavement when he wanted to. And right now, he wanted to.

Although he knew he'd regret it later, Gabe didn't bother to warm up. No stretches. No starting slow and working up to full stride. With Doofus loping joyfully beside him, he cut across the back of his property, jumped the creek at its narrowest point and hit the two-lane, little-used Farm Road that took him from town to country in less than a mile.

The Endicotts' cornfield was on his left, the Stuarts' okra and sweet potato patches on the right. This late in June the sweet corn stood only waist high and the okra was just beginning to put out shoots. But Gabe's thoughts that late June morning were about as far as they could get from calculating the economic impact of a good crop season for his constituents.

He'd managed to hang onto his cool when Suze calmly announced she intended to remain in uniform, give birth to their child, then flit in and out of its life for the next twelve or fifteen years. Or longer, if she made senior rank, as Gabe knew she would. She could extend her career to twenty-eight or thirty years, for God's sake!

While he sat here, in Cedar Creek. For the next twenty-eight or thirty…or fifty…years. That last number put a hitch in his stride. He almost stumbled as he squinted through the heat waves and saw his future stretch as straight and unchanging as the road ahead.

Doofus was sniffing at a dead crow on the side of the road but caught the sudden change in Gabe's rhythm. He contorted into a U, unwilling to abandon the fly-blown carcass but obviously wondering what his human was up to. When Gabe picked up his pace again, the dog unbent and happily resumed poking his nose into the rotting entrails.

By the time they'd circled around the Prestons' peach orchard and hit County Road 122, they were both swimming in sweat. Their route took them past a new development Gabe had worked his ass off to push through the zoning and planning committees. With five-acre lots and a sweeping view of the open fields to the south, Stony Brook Estates offered homeowners the wide-open spaces associated with country life but none of the rural inconveniences. All but two of the lots had sold, and the two- and three-hundred-thousand-dollar homes that had sprung up all had access to county and state-wide utilities. The tax revenue coming into the town from these new homes wasn't too shabby, either.

Another two miles brought them into older and more familiar territory. When they cut back across the creek behind Gabe's place, Doofus chose to splash and paddle to cool down, but Gabe opted for heeling off his running shoes and turning the garden hose on himself. Thinking his human was having more fun than he was, the dog danced around Gabe until they were both drenched.

To dry off, Gabe stretched out in one of the loungers on the vine-shaded flagstone patio. The same stones he'd damned near broken his back hauling in and muscling into place. With Doofus already on his back, belly exposed, legs splayed, Gabe thought about the next fifty years.

Since Ruby's was only a few blocks from her parents' house, Suze walked to her dinner meeting with Gabe. The moment she opened the front door, though, she almost turned and scooted out again. The place was jammed. Not surprising, considering how popular—and inexpensive—Ruby's specials were. Yet any hope that the café would constitute "neutral" ground evaporated when she faced a phalanx of curious stares.

Fighting the cowardly impulse to flee, she let the door whoosh shut behind her. A quick glance confirmed the café hadn't changed since her last visit two years ago. Hell, it hadn't changed all that much since her high school days. Granted, the Free WiFi sign taped to the old-fashioned cash register was a surprise. So was the Taylor Swift crossover hit competing with the dinner hour chatter. But tattered, leather-topped round stools still offered seats at the chipped Formica counter and the same square tables crowded the space between the counter and the row of booths lining the far wall.

Her throat tight, Suze remembered the times she and her friends had plopped down at the counter to stuff themselves on burgers and fries that beat the crap out of every fast-food spot within fifty miles. She remembered, too, all the occasions her family and Gabe's had pushed two or three of those tables together to accommodate an impromptu gathering. But the most vivid memories were of the times she'd huddled with Gabe in "their" booth. The last one in the row, just before the entrance to the kitchen and restrooms.

With the arrogant confidence of youth, they'd been so sure that the noise from the kitchen would drown out conversations that tended more and more toward X-rated as they progressed from adolescents to pre-teens to sex-hungry high schoolers. Looking back, Suze guessed those conversations had probably provided the folks around them with grins and outright guffaws.

She almost groaned when she spotted Gabe waiting for her in their booth. Before she could join him, though, she had to run the gauntlet.

"Suzanne! Heard you were back in town, girl. You gonna stay this time?"

She smiled at the owner of the only bookstore in town. The polar opposite of any rational being's image of a literary aficionado, Madelyn Winston was crude, rude to her customers and downed gin like it was water. But she'd kept Suze supplied with her favorite paperback novels all though school, many of which her mother would've been horrified to know she'd read.

"I'm on leave, Madelyn. Just taking a break."

"Will you be here this coming weekend?"

That came from Harry Peterman, the chubby, round-faced dentist who'd filled her cavities.

"I think so."

"That's great! We'll add you to the parade lineup. We love to include our very own hometown hero."

Too late Suze remembered that Dr. Peterman had headed the Fourth of July organizing committee for the past ten or fifteen years.

"I'm on leave," she told him. "I didn't bring my uniform."

"No problem. You can ride in the same convertible with Gabe. Everyone in town knows the two of you served in combat zones. Unless…uh…" Red flooded his chubby cheeks. "Sorry. I guess that might be a little uncomfortable for you."

"Just a little," she drawled.

"For pity's sake, Doc. Try for some class."

That came from Ruby herself. Suze couldn't begin to guess the café owner's age. Although a new crosshatch of wrinkles seemed to appear in her leathery skin every year, she sported the same red-orange hair and hoarse cigarette croak she'd always had.

"Hey, Ruby."

"Hey, Suzanne. Good to see you, girl."

"Thanks. You, too."

"Gabe's waiting for you." The proprietress angled

her chin toward the back of the café. "He's having the special. You?"

"Yes, please."

"Whadda you want to drink?"

"Try the featured cabernet," Madelyn advised. "It not bad for a Texas label. Not bad, at all."

"I'll stick to iced tea," Suze said with a smile…and immediately realized her mistake.

Heads turned. Brows rose. Glances zinged from patron to patron.

She observed the unspoken communications with a silent groan. She wasn't a boozer. Despite several notable youthful indiscretions, she'd never racked up anything even *close* to Madelyn's record of alcohol consumption. But apparently everyone from her book supplier to her dentist remembered that she enjoyed a glass of wine with dinner.

"Just tea," she reiterated. "Wouldn't be cool for the mayor's ex to get hauled into court for a DUI."

Keeping her smile plastered on, she skirted the tables and headed for the back of the café. When the occupant of the second booth jumped out and blocked her forward progress, she had no clue who he was. With a mumbled "'Scuse me," she tried to go around him.

"Suzanne! My God! Haven't seen you since high school."

"I'm sorry, I…"

"Dave Forrester. We sat next to each other in Advanced Physics."

"Dave? Good Lord, I wouldn't have…"

"Recognized me?" he finished on a laugh when she faltered. "I'm not surprised. I've put on a few pounds since then."

More than a few, she thought in amazement, although he carried the weight well. He'd been a skinny, freckle-faced runt in high school. His freckles were now almost lost in a deep butternut-tan attractively accented by sun-bleached blond hair and white squint lines at the corners of his eyes. Belatedly, Suze remembered Gabe telling her that Forrester was now a big honcho in the oil and gas business. Judging by his surprisingly rugged out-door appearance, the executive must still spend a good part of his time in the field. She gave him points for that.

"I heard you head your own company now, Dave."

"I do. Don't want to brag, but we made the Fortune 500 list last year."

"Good for you," Suze said, meaning it.

They'd been friends in high school, feeding off each other's passion for math and physics. Although Suze had sensed that her lab mate wanted to share more than a bench clamp and stringed cylinder, she'd been careful to signal neither interest nor encouragement. Only later did she learn that Gabe had underscored her effort with a direct and extremely blunt warning to Forrester to back the hell off.

She wasn't surprised that subliminal male rivalry had spilled over into a competitive race for mayor of Cedar Creek. And, she discovered a moment later, an apparent competition for the same woman.

Moving aside, Dave gestured to his dinner companion. "You remember Alicia, don't you?"

Damn! Crap! Sonova-freakin'-bitch.

Steeling herself, Suze pivoted to face her pixieish, violet-eyed nemesis. "Hey, Alicia."

"Hey, Suzanne." The smile was Colgate Ultra–bright.

"I asked Gabe to tell you hello from me when he and I talked last night."

"Oh, darn. He must've forgotten to give me the message."

The saccharine sweet reply shaved a few kilowatts off Prissy Missy's smile, but she never stayed dim for long. Her lips pursed into a dimpled pout that belied the bright glint in her eyes.

"I'll have to let him know what I think about that next time I see him."

"You do that." Hoping to hell there was no steam coming out of her ears, Suze nodded to Forrester. "Good to see you, Dave."

"You, too. Hey, listen. Last time I talked to Gabe, we were on opposite sides of the negotiating table 'bout cleanup at one of our wells. He let drop that you just worked a major spill at your base out in Arizona. If you've got time while you're home, I'd surely like to talk those pesky environmental issues with you." He fished in his hip pocket and extracted a heavily embossed business card from his wallet. "Give me a call. Maybe we can have lunch sometime."

"Maybe."

She tucked the card in her jeans pocket and was stopped twice more on her way to the back booth. Once by a friend of her father's, once by one of the servers who happened to be the grandson of her seventh grade math teacher, Very Scary Mrs. Lee.

"Gram is so proud of you," Tyler gushed. "She brags all the time about how you were her star pupil."

Suze blinked. That was news to her. Sharp featured and even sharper tongued, Very Scary had been relentless in her determination to pound advanced algebra into her students' heads. Everyone in her class had lived in dread of being called on to provide the answer to a homework problem.

"You should've seen Gram's face when she told me about that article," her teacher's eager grandson was saying. "The one in the *Daily Oklahoman* about you getting a Bronze Star medal. She said it's, like, a *big* deal."

"Well…"

"She's in the Gray Cedars Nursing Home now. If you have time while you're here, I know she'd love a visit."

"I'll sure stop by," Suze promised, meaning it. As intimidating as the math teacher had been, she'd pushed and prodded her students to their limits. Suze owed her scholarship to OU in no small part to the dedicated teacher's determination to see her students achieve their full potential.

By the time she finally reached the back of the diner, her mouth ached from forced smiles. "Lord," she muttered when she slid into the booth. "Looks like everyone in town still comes in for Ruby's sour cream chicken enchiladas."

"Pretty much. Did Doc Peterman tag you for the Fourth of July parade?"

"He tried, but I'm not ready to assume the hometown hero mantel."

"Why not? You earned that Bronze Star."

"Cedar Creek can boast more genuine heroes than me. You, for instance. Do I need to remind you that you logged more combat hours than I did before you separated?"

He didn't alter his lazy slouch against the back of the booth, but Suze could see the skin tighten across his cheekbones. "Let's not get into another debate over whether toggling a joystick to take out a target three thousand miles away qualifies as combat. I saw Dave Forrester give you his card. What's up with that?"

"He said you told him about the spill back at Luke. He wants to talk about those 'pesky' environmental issues involved in cleanup."

"About damn time he talked about them with someone who has some smarts!"

He shot a frown at the man now exiting the café. Suze craned around the edge of the bench in time to see Forrester loop a casually possessively arm around Alicia's waist.

She swung back around, her gaze locked on Gabe's as she heard the echo of his cool, flat comments this morning.

*It's over between him and Alicia. They shifted their friendship back into neutral.*

His decision? Or Alicia's? Suze couldn't help wondering as disgust underscored his next comment.

"The town council and I are fed up with his stall tactics. We're about two depositions away from suing his ass off."

"Whoa! That serious, is it?"

"I'll take you out to the Jones place, if you want. You can see the oil seepage on their property and..."

He broke off, wincing. "Hell! I can't believe I suggested that! Last thing you need is to risk the health of our baby by breathing in more toxic fumes."

Suze braced herself. Not the smoothest transition to the reason for this face-to-face but, abruptly, here they were.

Or not.

Smothering another curse, Gabe leaned toward her.

"Meeting here at Ruby's has to rank up with one of my stupidest ideas of all times. What do you say we get our dinners to go?"

"Okay by me."

He hooked a finger at their young server. "We'll take our two specials to go, Tyler."

"Sure thing, Mr. Mayor. I'll bag 'em right up for you." He turned a shy smile on Suze. "It was sure good to see you again, Captain. You won't forget to stop by and see Gram, will you?"

"I'll try to visit her tomorrow."

"She'll be totally jazzed to see you."

He was back within minutes with the two boxed and bagged dinners. "I put your drinks in the bags, too."

"Thanks. Tell Ruby to add the dinners on my tab."

"Sure will." He pocketed the generous tip Gabe passed him. "And thanks again for getting Shelby that summer job as a lifeguard. She's totally hyped about it."

"You're welcome."

"We're hoping this lifeguard job will help her turn the corner."

Suze waited until she and Gabe had rerun the gauntlet and exited into the evening heat to ask. "What corner does his sister Shelby need to turn?"

"She hooked up with the wrong crowd last year. Got bad into meth"

"Oh, no!"

The thought of the lively, inquisitive Shelby Lee glassy-eyed and stupid from drugs made Suze's heart hurt. It must have done the same to her steel-spined grandmother, the very scary Mrs. Lee.

"Shelby can't be more than, what? Sixteen?"

"Fifteen." With a light grip on her elbow, Gabe

steered her toward Ole Blue. "Jeff Hendricks found her stumbling along Route 9 three months ago and took her into custody. The kid was high out of her mind. Her folks can't afford private rehab, but we worked with DHS to get her into a state-sponsored program."

Suze didn't have any trouble substituting "I" for "we." That was Gabe to the core. Every one of his constituents, no matter how young or how old, could expect 150 percent from their mayor.

"How's she doing?"

"So far, so good."

When he opened Ole Blue's passenger door and she hoisted herself into the front seat, the cracked leather greeted her like an old friend. She refused to let herself think about the times she and Gabe had tussled on this same seat. Or the countless hours they'd steamed up the front windshield. Despite her best efforts, however, the memories wrapped around her like Saran Wrap as he deposited their dinners on the floor between them and backed out of the parking slot.

"Where are we going?" she asked, slanting him a quick look.

"Beats the hell out of me." He shifted into Drive. "You know any place we can escape our past and focus on the future?"

The question nicked an unexpected nerve. Stung, Suze had to remind herself that focusing on the future was the reason she'd driven all the way from Phoenix to Cedar Creek. Yet the fact that she was now carrying Gabe's child seemed to add to, not detract from their shared past. She didn't want to escape it. Not anymore. This small town with all its triumphs and tragedies formed a major part of their baby's heritage.

Thrown off-balance by the thought, Suze had no answer to his question. "I can't think of any place within a hundred miles."

They cruised Main with the scent of the spicy sour cream sauce tickling their nostrils. When Gabe cut right on 5th, then left on Poplar, she guessed where he was heading even before he made another turn. A short drive from there took them to the small park carved out of a bend in the creek. The tiny green space was just big enough for a swing set, two picnic tables and a pebbled walk along the creek bank. A historical marker indicated that the town's first settler, Jacob Neumann, had registered a claim to this quarter section on April 22, 1889—the same day of the land run—and subsequently donated the land for this stamp-sized little park.

The tiny retreat was far enough off the town's main streets to give at least an illusion of privacy. As an added plus, the park's thick canopy of trees provided cooling shade from the early evening sun. Buzzing cicadas and the sluggish ripple of the creek sounded familiar refrains as Suze and Gabe claimed a table tucked under a massive, scaly-barked sycamore.

"This is better," he said as he opened the sack. "*Much* better."

"Still neutral territory," Suze agreed, "but at least we can talk without interruption. And eat," she added as Gabe extracted a half-dozen takeout containers, along with plastic utensils, straws and paper napkins.

Once the cartons were opened, drinks distributed, and utensils unwrapped, she dug in. The special was even more delicious than she remembered. Soft, still-warm flour tortillas wrapped around spicy shredded chicken and cheese and onions. A creamy white sauce flavored with red and green chilies topped the fat enchiladas. The accompanying beans were done Okie style, whole pinto instead of mashed and refried, and Ruby always seemed to throw half a garden's worth of chopped carrots, corn and green onions in each serving of Spanish rice.

Suze downed almost half her enchilada before glancing across the picnic table to see Gabe watching her with a glint of amusement in his hazel eyes. "You always did like the Wednesday special."

"It's my fave."

He gestured toward her stomach with his fork. "Hope the baby likes all that spicy stuff, too."

"He's been pretty tolerant so far. I've been tired and draggy at times, but no morning sickness."

"He?"

"Or she. I alternate genders at will."

"That's what my sisters did, too, until they learned the sex. Sometime around the third or fourth month, I think."

"That's the normal time frame." Suze poked at her beans, then forced herself to meet his eyes. "The doc talked to me about a noninvasive prenatal blood test at ten weeks. They check for Down syndrome and a few other chromosomal conditions. They can also look for bits of Y chromosome in my blood to see if I'm carrying a boy or a girl."

"Let's talk about that."

He was so calm. So steady. So *Gabe*. Just being able to share all this with him almost got Suze hormonal again.

"You said your family practice doc found no evidence of toxic infiltration in your blood or lungs."

"Right."

"And you've been to a GYN for a prenatal check?"

"Right. And all tests came back normal."

"But you're still worried."

"Hell, yes, I'm worried. No, make that scared. This whole baby business has pretty well rocked me off my rails. I haven't quite figured out all the necessary accommodations and changes to my lifestyle yet."

"*Our* lifestyles, Suze. We have to figure out the necessary changes to *our* lifestyles. I want to be part of it, start to finish."

"Well, you were certainly there at the start."

She stabbed at the last of her enchilada but a need to lay the truth bare stilled her hand. She laid the fork down, slowly, carefully, and met her husband's eyes.

"It's your baby, Gabe. In case you were wondering."

"I wasn't."

"We can do a blood test."

"No."

"That way you won't ever doubt it."

"No."

"Just think about…"

"Dammit, Suze. I don't need a blood test. You said I'm the father. That's enough for me. It's always been enough."

The air went out of her with a soft whoosh. Her shoulders slumped, her chest caved. And the stupid, *stupid* tears burned her eyes again.

"Sorry," she muttered. "No morning sickness so far, but my emotions are jumping up, down and every way but sideways."

"Hey, I've got eleven nieces and nephews, remember? My brothers-in-law can tell stories about out-of-whack hormones that would make any sane man run for the hills."

"So, why aren't you running?"

"My kid. My wife. My life."

"Ex-wife." She sniffed. "Ex."

"Yeah, well…"

He swung a leg over his bench, came around to her side of the table. When he sat down again and opened his arms, Suze fell into them as naturally as if she'd never left them.

"Here's the thing," he said, his chin rubbing back and forth against her temple. "I took Doofus for a long run after you left this morning. All the way out to the Endicotts' place and back again."

That had to be eight or nine miles. Suze would've commented on his endurance if she wasn't still swimming in hormonal soup.

"I did some heavy thinking after the mutt and I hosed down."

"And?"

"And every thought circled back to the only thing that that's ever mattered to me."

He curled a knuckle, tipped up her chin. The sun had slanted well down below the tree line now. Shadows played across his face, made even more hazy by the stupid tears that still blurred her eyes.

"I think we should undo the *ex*."

"What?"

"Marry me, Suzanne. Again."

Stunned, she jerked upright. "You're kidding!"

"Never been more serious in my life."

The magic of the moment dissolved in a hard, sharp hurt. As quick as that, they were back to where they'd been three years ago. The only game changer was the baby. Gabe had itched to put down roots. She'd thrived on the excitement and fulfillment of her job.

And never the twain shall meet.

"So we get married again," she said, her voice thick with unshed tears. "We add another room onto your house for a nursery. Raise our little prince or princess and their brothers and sisters here in Cedar Creek. You'll coach their T-ball games and teach them history. And I'll... I'll... Hmm. I guess I could work for Dave Forrester. He needs someone to help clean up his environmental messes."

"That's one scenario," Gabe said gruffly, refusing to let her pull out of his arms. "Here's another. We get married again. I go back to Phoenix with you. We have this baby together and any others that come along. Then, someday, if it's right for both of us, we may—or may not—come back to Cedar Creek."

For the second time in as many minutes, he'd yanked the rug right out from under her. Stunned, Suze leaned back in the circle of his arms. "How can you move to Phoenix? Your teaching job is here. And in case you've forgotten, you're the mayor of Cedar Creek."

"Remember Joanna Hicks?"

"Who's Joanna...? Wait! Isn't she the bodybuilder? The one who competed for Mrs. Oklahoma some years back?"

"That's her."

Suze could still remember the publicity stills Ms. Hicks's proud husband had plastered all over town. Joanna Hicks must've been in her fifties at that time, and according to Suze's mother, she and every other woman in Cedar Creek would've killed for those rippling deltoids and flat abs. To the entire town's delight, Ms. Hicks walked away with the crown.

"Joanne's the senior member of the town council," Gabe related. "She can step in as mayor without missing a beat."

"But... But you're so good at it. Everyone says so. They also say your next step should be to run for state or national office."

He brushed that off with a careless shrug. "Maybe I will. Someday. Right now all that matters is you and our baby."

"What about your job? You love teaching."

"Last I heard, they had high school teachers in Arizona. And they pay them a damn sight more than they pay here in Oklahoma."

"Right. As if you do it for the money!" Her mind whirled. "What about certification? And afterward? When the baby's born? If I get transferred to another state?"

"You'll be on restricted duty, so for at least a year you won't be deploying or pulling remote duty. Plenty of time for us to figure out what happens afterwards."

She struggled to gather her chaotic thoughts. "Gabe, you don't really mean this. You can't."

"Yeah, I do."

He brushed his mouth over hers. Once. Again.

"I won't lie to you. I love Cedar Creek. Almost as much as I love living within shouting distance of our families. But they haven't been able to patch the jagged hole in my heart these past three years. You're the only one who can do that, Susie Q. You and our baby."

## Chapter Seven

When they'd finished their dinners and bagged the trash, Suze was still in a daze. She'd driven all the way from Phoenix hoping to work out an amicable custody sharing agreement. Her ex's astounding offer to jettison his home, his family and both his careers had turned her world upside down.

He'd meant it, though. Every word. If his dead-serious expression hadn't convinced her, that achingly tender kiss would have. As light as the touch had been, her lips still tingled and her heart fluttered thinking about the promise behind it.

She struggled to gather her chaotic thoughts as they drove out of the park. The plan was to break the news about the baby to their respective families. But Suze needed more time. More thought.

"Let's go to your place," she suggested. "We can

talk to our folks tomorrow. We should keep tonight just for us."

"I was wondering how long we'd have to make nice before I could waltz you away from our respective families and into bed."

Whoa! There was nothing light or tender about that declaration. Or the quick, fast grin he shot her way. Her hormones took off again, and this time they catapulted her straight out of confusion and into lust.

By the time they pulled into Gabe's front drive, heat was racing through her veins. Even with her pulse tripping a mile a minute, she had to battle a sudden wave of guilt as she took in the gorgeously renovated homestead.

"Oh, Gabe. You've put so much work into this place. How can you give it up?"

"We'll rent it out. Or sell it. It's just a house, Suze. A place."

They heard Doofus's sonic booms before they climbed out of Ole Blue. Gabe slammed the truck door, frowning. "We'll have to figure out what to do with him, though. I doubt the neighbors at your condo would appreciate his vocal tendencies. Maybe one of my sisters can take him."

He meant that, too, Suze realized with another jab of guilt. He was really serious about packing up and leaving his life here behind. The reality of it humbled her.

"We're not going to palm Doofus off on your sisters. He's weird, but a fun kind of weird. My condo lease is up in six months. We can find another place to live. Somewhere with several layers of soundproofing inside and plenty of space for him to run outside."

That potential problem resolved, she accepted the hound's ecstatic welcome. "We're going to be besties," she informed him. "And when the baby comes, you'll have to pull extra shifts on guard duty."

The prospect didn't appear to worry Doofus. Suze and Gabe waited at the screen door while he made a rapid circuit of the front yard, watered four of his favorite bushes and bounded back. His claws clicked a happy staccato as he pranced down the entry hall ahead of them. Suze's heart thumped to the same beat, then kicked into double-time when Gabe caught her elbow and tugged her around.

No soft brush of his lips this time. No gentle acknowledgement of their recommitment to each other. His mouth locked onto hers. Hard and hungry and demanding an instant response. She gave it eagerly, fiercely, and barely noticed when the dog charged back down the hall to get in on the action. Gabe pushed him away, or tried to. Finally gave up and admitted temporary defeat.

"The bedroom's upstairs. I'll feed this guy, which should lower his energy to a more manageable level, then come on up."

Suze had no trouble locating the master bedroom suite. The oak-tread staircase opened directly onto it. Gabe had knocked out the walls up here, too, she saw with an admiring glance. Gone were the dime-sized bedrooms that characterized most early Oklahoma territorial homesteads. What was left was a clean, uncluttered space with skylights that opened the sloping roof to the swiftly darkening night sky and a king-size bed positioned for a perfect view of the stars.

The master bath was just as spacious, Suze saw when she ducked in to use the john and wash off the residue of the dog's effusive greeting. Another skylight let in the light and would sound a noisy tattoo during Oklahoma's frequent hail storms, she suspected. Still, the prospect of lying beside Gabe and watching lightning flash across the sky above them was almost as seductive as the idea of curling against him under a blanket of stars.

The guilt rushed back. This was his home. He'd put so much of his heart and soul into it. How selfish, how *wrong*, was she to give up so little when he proposed to give up so much?

Then Gabe came up the stairs, shedding his shirt and barking a stern command over his shoulder in the process. "Stay! Right where you are. I mean it, Doofus!"

Suze flipped off the bathroom lights and met him in the middle of the room. Enough moonglow now spilled through the skylights to wrap him in soft light and dark shadows. Hunger curled in her belly as she ran her palms over his shoulders, his upper arms, his chest. His biceps bunched at her touch. His pecs went rock hard.

Did that deep-throated purr come from her? That low, vibrating hum? She didn't know. Didn't care. Hunger for this man, for *her* man, consumed her. This was her mate. The man she'd chosen. Claimed as her own before God and their families and damned near half the town. She'd claim him again, Suze thought fiercely. Tomorrow. But tonight there was just Gabe and her and the bed that beckoned like a safe port in a storm.

They took their time. Heeling out of sandals and shoes. Unsnapping and peeling down jeans. Disposing of extraneous items. And exploring each new patch of bared skin with eyes and hands and mouths.

Gabe forced himself to go slowly. Gently. His sisters had once embarrassed the hell out of him with an impromptu discussion of their heightened sex drive during their pregnancies. He did his damnedest to block their respective spouses' too-frank comments from his mind by focusing on the fact that this was Suze. His Suze. And it was their baby she was carrying. He'd cut off both arms and a leg before he'd do anything that might harm either of them.

Still, his lungs burned with the effort of holding back. He gritted his teeth. Waited until she opened for him and rose to meet his slow thrust. His jaw still locked, he harnessed his hunger until she clamped her calves around his and drove to a shuddering, spine-arching climax. Then he tangled his fingers in hers, pinned the backs of her hands to the mattress beside her head and let the pleasure sweep over him in hot, dark waves.

Wrung dry and damned near catatonic, he collapsed beside her. His breath was harsh and rough, hers a soft, ragged sigh. They lay side by side while the sweat cooled on their skin and the sky above them darkened to night.

"Gabe."

He could barely manage a grunt when she poked an elbow into his ribs.

"Gabe, wake up. I need to call my folks and tell them I won't be home tonight. Unless…"

"Unless nothing." His brains hadn't totally unscrambled but he had no trouble interpreting the question behind her hesitation. "We're back where we belong, Susie Q. In bed. Together. Tell your folks we'll explain tomorrow."

"I doubt they'll need much of an explanation but…" She poked him again. "Pass me my phone."

With another muffled grunt, Gabe rolled onto his

side. Her jeans were too far away to reach so he retrieved the phone from his. At which point he discovered Doofus crouched at the top of the stairs. The dog's eyes gleamed in the moonlight and his snout was flattened against the hardwood flooring. When he saw his human show signs of life, he gave a pitiful whine.

"Stay where you are," Gabe commanded sternly as he snagged his jeans and fished out the phone. "Right where you are."

Another whine, even more desolate that the last, brought Suze up on one elbow. "Am I usurping his side of the bed?"

"You are, but he'll have to get used to it."

"Poor baby," she cooed to the mournful watcher.

"Don't give him any encouragement!"

The warning came too late. Translating her sympathy into an invitation, Doofus launched himself across the room and took a joyful leap. When he landed in the middle of the bed, Suze laughed and scooted over to make room for him.

"I warned you," Gabe said in mock disgust as he handed her the phone. "Your folks are on speed dial. Just hit five."

When her mom answered, she didn't comment on the fact that Gabe's number must've come up on caller ID but she almost choked when Suze said she wouldn't be home that night. Then staunch, upright, church deacon Mary Elizabeth Kingfisher Jackson chuckled and issued a delighted invitation.

"Why don't you and Gabe come for breakfast?"

Suze mouthed the question at the man beside her. His response was to tug the phone out of her hand.

"We'll be there, Mary. And if you should feel inclined to make your world-famous blueberry pecan pancakes, I'd be real grateful."

"I think I can manage that."

"That went well," Suze commented drily when he cut the connection. "If she makes you pancakes for fooling around with your ex-wife, just think what she'll cook up when we tell about the baby."

"We'll eat extremely well for the foreseeable future," Gabe said smugly. "Speaking of which…" He propped himself up and aimed a stern finger at the foot of the bed. "Off, Doofus. Now."

The dog tried to burrow in but Gabe was relentless. "Off. The. Bed."

Looking aggrieved, the hound wiggled backward on his haunches and just sort of slithered off the end, taking the rolled-back comforter with him.

"Back to the foreseeable future." Still propped on one elbow, Gabe rested a hand on Suze's sheet-covered belly. "How long can we let your mom feed us?"

"How long can I stay, you mean? I'm on two weeks' leave but I took my time getting here." She laid her hand atop his. "So we have another eight days, Gabe. Nine at most."

"Plenty of time for your mom and mine to get a head start on fattening you up. The baby and I will take it from there. Now we'd better get some sleep. We've got a busy nine days ahead."

Suze's parents took the news that their daughter and her former husband were getting back together exactly as she'd anticipated. Her dad whooped and pounded Gabe on the back. Her mom laughed and cried at the same time. They greeted the news that they were going to be grandparents even more ecstatically.

"Oh, Suzanne! You can't imagine how happy this makes us. When are you due? I need to start planning a baby shower."

"Not until February."

"Perfect. We'll have it in January and do a snow-flake theme. I saw the cutest decorations on Pinterest the other day. Have you told your mom yet, Gabe? I want to get her and your sisters in on the planning, too."

"Not yet. We're going to see her after we leave here."

"Well, then, my gracious. Let's feed you so you can get over there!"

Still beaming, she led the way into the kitchen. The round glass table was already set with cheerful yellow placemats and her mom's favorite mishmash of china. A lone sunflower poked its head from a chipped pitcher.

With the ease of long habit, the four of them divided the labor. Suze popped slices of wheat bread in the toaster, her dad pan-grilled thick slices of Canadian bacon and her mom poured the prepared batter onto a griddle. Gabe did his part by filling the juice glasses.

Once they were all seated and digging in, her mom wanted to know about the wedding. "When do you want to have it and who shall we invite?"

Suze and Gabe exchanged glances. They'd tossed around various options and had agreed on one that worked best for them, given the circumstances.

"We did the big church wedding last time, Mom. This time around we're going for quick and easy. We plan to detour to Vegas on our way to back to Arizona and get married there."

"Oh, no! You're not going to go through one of those tacky, drive-up chapels."

"No, ma'am. Suze has a friend who works out there. Since we've got so little time, we thought we'd call her and ask her to set it up for us."

"Why so little time?" Her mother angled her head with its turquoise-tipped bob. "You've got months to do this right. Why not wait a few weeks and have a nice, quiet celebration with your families when Suze gets out of the service and moves back to Cedar Creek?"

"I'm not separating from the service, Mom, or moving back. Gabe's moving to Arizona."

Confusion blanked the faces of both her parents. They exchanged surprised glances, and it was her hardworking, traditional, nose-to-the-grindstone dad who posed the inevitable questions.

"But your job, Gabe? Your responsibilities as mayor?"

"School's out for the summer. The school board has plenty of time to find a replacement. And Joanna Hicks can handle the town council until or unless they decide to hold a special election."

"What about your house? You've worked so hard on it. Surely you're not going to let it just stand empty?"

"I'll rent it out until we see what happens after the baby comes."

Her folks were raising the same objections Suze had, and Gabe was answering with the same calm certainty. But the guilt came back and made the blueberries in her pancakes suddenly taste too tart.

Still, she'd offered him the chance to be part of their child's life without completely uprooting his own. Getting remarried and moving to Arizona had been his idea, after all.

"What *will* happen after the baby comes?" Her mom wanted to know. "I'm assuming you won't have to deploy while you're pregnant, Suzanne, but what about afterward?" Her anxious glance went from her daughter to her former son-in-law and back again. "You two split up because of all the separations and, well…all those separations. How is adding a baby to that mix going to make it any easier?"

"I've changed," Gabe answered calmly. "So has Suze. We're different people now, Mary, with very different priorities."

Suze knew he'd never told his in-laws the precise reasons behind his decision to separate from the Air Force. Only she knew how much launching lethal drone strikes from thousands of miles away had played on his conscience. Her folks had just assumed, as had the rest of their friends and family, that since his marriage had fallen apart just as he was finishing his service commitment, he'd come home to heal.

Now he was thrusting himself back into the military environment. Not as an officer this time. Not as a war fighter. As a military spouse. It would be a completely different and challenging role for him.

A new role for her, too. She'd worked with enough other military woman to know how tough it was to combine wife, mother and warrior. Suze would need to adjust her career goals and assignment preferences to accommodate her family.

Gabe sure was right about different priorities.

His mom pretty much mirrored her parents' reactions. Violet was thrilled that Gabe and Suze were together again, overjoyed to hear about the baby and shocked that her son's life was taking such an abrupt one-eighty.

She didn't question their decision, though. Violet had lost her husband when he was in his forties and pretty much raised her four children on her own. If nothing else, she'd taught them to make their own choices in life.

"She looks so frail." Suze worried when they left. Her mother-in-law's limp had added to her growing guilt. "The hip replacement must've taken a lot out of her."

"It did. I've tried to talk her into moving in with me. So have Jill and Dave. Penny and Lyle even offered to build one of those snazzy mother-in-law retreats behind their house. But mom's determined to remain queen of her own castle."

A little more of Suze's joy had seeped away with each of these encounters. Dinner at his middle sister's house that evening pretty well drained it. Penny and Jill and their spouses were there, along with Kathy's husband, Don. Kathy was pulling midnights at the big new healthplex that served Mustang, Cedar Creek and surrounding communities. Of all Gabe's family, Kathy had been the most unforgiving. She'd made no secret of the fact that she blamed the demands of Suze's military career for the divorce—totally ignoring the long hours she herself put in and the many emergencies she responded to as a critical care nurse.

The sisters and spouses present voiced the same hearty congratulations at the news that Gabe and Suze were getting back together. And the same incredulous surprise that he intended to leave Cedar Creek to take up duties as a househusband. By the time Suze and Gabe left, her emotions were all over the place again.

"Dammit!" She gripped her hands in her lap and

glared through Ole Blue's windshield at the leafy oaks twisting and bending in the breeze. "I woke up so happy this morning. Now all I want to do is run away from home. *Again*."

"No running this time, kid. For you or for me."

She angled in her seat. "We screwed up so badly last time, Gabe. How do we know we're not screwing up again?"

"We don't."

"It's not just us this time," she said with a touch of desperation as he turned in to the curving drive. "As everyone we've talked to today has pointed out, we're adding a baby to the equation."

"We're adding more than a baby," he said wryly as the twin spears of Ole Blue's headlights initiated a booming chorus from Doofus.

"I'm serious. Maybe we need to rethink this whole thing. Maybe we're making another mistake and... Whoa!"

She slapped a palm against dash to brace herself as Gabe hit the brakes and jammed Ole Blue into Park. Without saying a word, he killed the engine. Then he shouldered open his door and marched around the hood. Yanking open her door, he reached across her to unclip her seat belt and almost dragged her out of the truck.

"This is not a mistake."

*This* being the hard kiss he laid on her.

"Neither is this."

Scooping her up, he took the front steps in two swift strides. He had to balance her on his knee to unlock the front door, then scoot sideways when Doofus burst out. The dog was still emitting a vociferous welcome when

Gabe let the screen door slam and kicked the front door shut behind him.

His muscles were taut, his stride swift as he hit the stairs. Moments later, Suze was stretched on the bed where she'd wakened to such sleepy, all-pervasive joy a mere fourteen hours ago.

"Forget Vegas," he told her, popping the buttons on his shirt. "We're heading to the county courthouse tomorrow and forking over fifty bucks for a marriage license. Since Oklahoma doesn't require blood tests or a waiting period, I'll get Judge Porter to marry us."

"And I don't have any say in this plan?"

"Yeah, you do. Two words. I do. Now shut up and kiss me, Captain."

So she did.

And would've done a whole lot more if Doofus hadn't chorused his eagerness to rejoin the party. Gabe muttered an oath and went downstairs to let him in. When the two of them came back upstairs, Suze welcomed her soon-to-be husband with open arms.

The Canadian County Courthouse was housed in a low, sand-colored building on Choctaw Avenue in El Reno, Oklahoma. Part of the Oklahoma City Metropolitan statistical area, the county ranked as the fifth most populous in the state. As such, it did a booming business in marriage licenses. The clerk was friendly and efficient. Gabe's driver's license and Suze's military ID satisfied the age and identification requirements. Since Gabe knew the question of their current marital status would come up, he also presented their divorce decree.

"As you may know," the clerk explained, "divorced persons can't marry anyone other than their previous spouse for a period of six months. But," she continued as she skimmed the court documents, "it looks like you're good on that count. As you also know, the normal fee is fifty dollars. Only five if you had premarital counseling."

"Our pastor did the counseling the first time around," Suze confirmed. "The certificate should be on file."

"Hang on, let me scroll back to the original license."

Now that she thought about it, Suze had to admit that premarital counseling should probably be an even more stringent requirement for couples who failed miserably the first time around. Luckily for her and Gabe, it was not.

"Yep, there it is. Okay, folks, five dollars and you're on your way."

When Gabe handed her the bill, she printed out the license and passed it across the counter with a pointed reminder. "It's good for ten days."


"Ten days," Suze echoed as she and Gabe crossed the sun-baked parking lot. "That's two more than we have left in Cedar Creek. Think we can do everything that needs doing in just over a week?"

Gabe slanted her an amused glance. "This from the woman who maintains three separate go-kits and can clamber up the ramp of a C-17 with less than five hours notice?"

"That's different."

"What's different? You get the word, you pack up, you go." Grinning, he dropped a kiss on her nose. "Besides, we're not exactly charting unfamiliar ground here, woman. You. Me. A marriage license. A promise to hang on. This time," he added, his expression and his voice going dead serious, "forever."

"This time forever," she echoed.

Yielding to her mother's fervent pleas, they'd asked their pastor to conduct the marriage ceremony. Suze had spoken to him personally, explained it would be a private ceremony with only immediate family in attendance. They'd settled on four o'clock the same afternoon they obtained the license.

That presented Suze with another dilemma. She hadn't packed anything suitable for a re-wedding, and she didn't think her folks would appreciate the irony of her sparkly, one-of-a-kind Warrior Mom T-shirt. So, after she and Gabe got back to the house, she jumped in her T-bird and made a quick excursion to Penn Square Mall in Oklahoma City.

The mall catered to the wealthy, oil-money suburbs that surrounded it and included plenty of high-end stores. With time so short, however, Suze zipped into Dillards and took the escalator to the second floor. Luckily, she spotted the perfect dress on an end cap right as she got off the escalator. A soft, summery chiffon in misty blue, it featured a wide belt in supple, cream-colored leather. The matching floppy-brimmed hat trimmed with white roses was an added bonus. She grabbed the hat, found the dress in her size and darted into a dressing room. Her purchases in hand, she hit the shoe department and scored a pair of Donald Pilner sling-backs in the same creamy leather as the belt.

She kept to the speed limit on the way back to Cedar Creek and got home with just enough time to shower, blow-dry her hair and slap on some lip gloss. Wearing her wedding finery, she went downstairs to find Gabe waiting for her. He'd gone with a dark suit, a gray shirt with a satiny sheen and an amber tie that made his hazel eyes look more gold than green.

As they drove to the church, Suze couldn't help thinking that the contrast between this occasion and their first wedding. She and her mom and her best friend had spent months planning and organizing that one.

It took place the day after she and Gabe graduated from OU and been commissioned as second lieutenants in the Air Force. So, so proud of their bright, shiny lieutenant's bars, Suze had chosen to wear her formal mess dress uniform instead of a wedding gown. The starched, pleated white blouse. The midnight-blue jacket with its silver officer's braid banding the cuff. The matching long skirt slit up to her knee. Gabe had worn his uniform, too. And their friends from OU's Reserve Officer Commissioning Program had raised their sabers to form an arch when the bride and groom exited the church.

No uniforms this time around. No arch. But the church was the same. Still small, still painted a blistering white, its steeple standing proud against a bright, searing sky. The congregation was minuscule compared to that of Oklahoma's huge cathedrals, Suze knew. Only about two hundred worshipers, most of whom knew or were related to each other. And the pastor's sermons often took a tilt to the left…surprising considering how deep they were in the Bible Belt.

Roses had filled every niche and cranny of the sanctuary for their first wedding. Friends and family had crammed the pews. Her bridesmaids wore shimmering lilac silk, and Gabe's groomsmen had formed solid phalanx. Their flower girl had tripped, Suze recalled with a smile, and spilled her basket of rose petals. The four-year-old's heartbroken wails had brought Gabe from his post at the altar, and his teary-eyed niece was still clinging to his hand when Suze floated down the aisle.

She didn't float this time. Her footsteps dragging, she approached the church door with a touch of dread. The thought of standing at the same altar, repeating the vows they'd already broken once, suddenly struck her as tempting fate just a little too much.

"Why did I let my mom talk us into this?" she muttered.

"Because you love her, and she loves you."

She pulled him to a stop. "There's still time, Gabe. We could delay this. Head for Vegas."

"We could. Or we could share this moment with our families, like we've shared every other significant event in our lives."

She made a face. "Have I ever told you that you really piss me off sometimes?"

"Yeah, babe," he answered, laughing. "You have. So are we going to do this or not?"

"I guess so."

Still grinning, he opened the door. Suze took one step inside and stopped cold.

The small sanctuary wasn't crammed. Flowers didn't burst from dozens of vases. No lilac-robed maids of honor or uniformed groomsmen waited for them at the altar. But family and their closest friends filled at least half the pews. Gabe's sister Penny waited at the door to hand her a small bouquet of white roses. And little Tildy gave a delighted yelp.

"Uncle Gabe!"

The girl wiggled off her mom's lap, snatched up a

wicker basket and promptly spilled its contents. When she scooped up a handful of petals and threw them at the new arrivals with the force of a future left fielder, Kathy sent her once and future sister-in-law a droll glance. "Déjà vu all over again."

The perfect theme for the occasion, Suze thought with a wry grin.

She and Gabe. Second time around. Firmly suppressing her last flickers of guilt and doubt, she re-joined her life to his.

It all seemed so surreal until she slid his ring on his finger—again. He'd taken it off after the divorce but kept it. She'd kept hers, too. The wide band of etched white gold was in her safety deposit box back in Phoenix. To her surprise, Gabe had somehow found the time to purchase a circlet of channel-cut diamonds set in the same white gold.

"You can wear it above your original ring," he said as he slipped the circlet over her knuckle. "Seems pretty appropriate for a twice-married bride."

A moment later it was done. They were husband and wife.

Again.

Suze should've been lost in the sweeping joy of the moment. Instead, she found herself folding her left hand into a fist and making a fierce, silent vow. Despite the uncertainties and challenges ahead, this ring wasn't going into any safety deposit box.

## Chapter Eight

Their first honeymoon had been a week at an all-inclusive resort in Mexico, a gift from their collective family members. Their second consisted of a celebratory supper at Ruby's with family and friends, followed by a quick trip to move Suze's things from her parents' house to Gabe's.

Their second wedding night, however, more than matched that of the first. They were older, wiser and much more appreciative of what they'd let slip through their fingers. The loving was slow, sweet, each kiss a reminder, each touch a promise.

Stars winked above the skylights when they were done, but it was still early enough for Gabe to take Doofus for the run he so desperately wanted and Suze to indulge in an extended soak in the modern version of a claw-foot tub that dominated the master bath. With its slightly inclined back and extra-long length, it fit her perfectly.

After her soak, she pulled on a pair of shorts and her Warrior Mom T-shirt, then stretched out on one of the patio loungers while she waited for Gabe to return. Bullfrogs bellowed their love songs from the creek, and the distant boom and pop of firecrackers signaled that folks were getting a head start on the upcoming Fourth of July weekend.

Gabe and Doofus joined her on the patio, both sweaty from their run. He was chugging from a bottle of water and took time to splash water into the hound's outdoor bowl before plopping down in the lounger next to Suze's.

"Damned idiots," he muttered as a starburst of red, white and blue exploded above the tree line. "We've banned firecrackers inside town limits. Outside, though, there's plenty of open space to shoot off Roman candles and spinners. And plenty of idiots who'll end up at the ER when the things explode in their faces."

"C'mon," Suze teased. "How many bottle rockets did you and your pals shoot off when you were kids?"

"Too many. It was pure dumb luck that none of us lost fingers or an eye. But they were legal back then."

He frowned as another boom carried through the trees. Seconds later a rocket trailing green stars arced across the night sky.

"The problem is, it's been so dry lately. We were close to record low precipitation for the month of June. Half the county is a tinderbox just waiting for a spark. The chief's got all of his full-time and most of us volunteer firefighters on standby."

"You're one of the volunteers?"

"I signed on when I moved back home. The training was brutal," he admitted. "Probably not as bad as what you combat engineers go through, but I must have sweated off a good ten pounds in that turnout gear."

Firefighters in Air Force units were integral members of the Civil Engineering Squadron. Suze had participated in enough training exercises and emergency responses with them to appreciate the grit and determination it took to qualify, even as a volunteer.

When another starburst lit the sky, Gabe swore again. "I wish our state legislators had the balls to outlaw sale of fireworks to individuals. God knows I've harangued enough of them about it."

"Maybe you should've run for state senator instead of mayor," she joked.

"I thought about it. Might still do it someday."

The answer didn't surprise her. She knew Gabe was passionate about politics on the national level. They both were. But their military duties precluded any kind of active participation in political campaigns or issues.

So when her mom relayed the news that he'd been elected mayor, Suze had realized she should've expected Gabe to get involved. He was too smart, too active, to channel all his energy into teaching and coaching. Especially, she thought on an inner grimace, with no wife or kids to otherwise distract him.

He made a good mayor. Everyone said so. He'd make a good state senator. And maybe, in time, lieutenant governor or governor. The thought that he was shelving the idea took some of the sparkle from their starlit wedding night.

He put it back in after he abandoned the evening to the bullfrogs, adjourned to the shower and joined her in bed. Suze would never again take for granted the simple joy of having her husband lean over her, his shoulders blocking the moon's glow and his eyes dark pools as he stroked her tummy.

"Guess we need to start thinking about names," he murmured between strokes.

"Mmm. Better leave it to me. You're not exactly a wizard in the name department."

"Hey. Jill liked Matilda when I suggested it."

"Right. Jilly and Tildy. Obviously, Jill didn't think that one all the way through. And Doofus?"

The dog's ears shot up at the sound of his name. Once again, he'd been banished from the bed but was only waiting for anything that sounded even remotely like an invitation to reclaim his half of the mattress.

He remained banished, however, and no grass or roof fires erupted during the night to launch Cedar Creek's volunteer fire department into action.

Suze and Gabe used the next couple of days to inventory the house and sort out what would stay, what would go into storage and what would go with them. They were ready to start packing the boxes stacked in various rooms but had decided to hold off until after the Fourth of July celebrations. Gabe had too much to do to get ready for the parade, their family picnic afterward and the fireworks display that night to focus on packing.

The call came just as he and Suze were finishing breakfast. She was still in the oversize T-shirt she used as a sleepshirt. Gabe was in sweats and getting ready to take Doofus for his morning run. He answered, listened for a moment, then told the caller he'd be right there.

"What's happening?" she asked when he disconnected with a smothered oath.

"The crew setting up the reviewing stand for the parade somehow managed to puncture the K-6."

It had been a while since she'd submitted a study of
central Oklahoma's water treatment and distribution
systems as part of her hydraulics engineering course.
She remembered enough, however, to know Cedar
Creek's K-6 was one of two major arteries leading from
the primary pumping station to a network of secondary
mains. With the K-6 shut down, half the town wouldn't
be able to wash their breakfast dishes or water their
lawns. Or, she thought grimly, raise enough water pressure to respond to fires at the far ends of the branch.

"I did that hydraulics study in college," she reminded
Gabe. "It's probably way out of date now, but…do you
want me to come check out the break with you?"

"Yes! No," he amended in the next breath. "My guys
alerted the county water management board. Their
emergency response crew is on the way. Much as I
could use your expertise, one of us needs to be here for
the walk-through with Alicia."

"Riiight."

Gabe had already grabbed his keys and green ballcap
with Mayor embroidered across the crown.

"She's the best Realtor in the area, Suze, and she's
heading out of town this afternoon to spend the rest of
the weekend at some posh resort with Dave Forrester.
If we're going to get the house listed for rent before we
head to Arizona, we need to get the walk-through done
this morning."

Like Little Miss Priss needed a walk-through, Suze
thought snidely. She probably already knew everything

from the alarm system code to which side of the bed the owner slept on. Smothering the nasty thought, she flapped a hand.

"No problem. I've got it covered. Go!"

Still, it left a funny taste in her mouth when Gabe rushed off to handle an emergency that fell smack into *her* area of expertise. She hadn't just studied water distribution systems in college. Air Force Prime BEEF teams dug wells, repaired pipes and, in their humanitarian response role, had to handle all kinds of disasters. Suze remembered all too clearly jumping into a sewage-filled trench in earthquake-ravaged Ecuador to help her grunting, straining troops wrestle a new section of pipe into place. It had taken them days to scrub the stink from their boots and uniforms.

No stink for her today, she decided. No baggy uniform, either. By the time Alicia rang the bell an hour later and catapulted Doofus into a frenzy, Suze had washed and dried her hair, liberally applied the few cosmetics she'd brought with her and wiggled into jeans that clung to a butt that was still pretty damned trim, if she did say so herself. Her yellow 56th Fighter Wing T-shirt was a little faded from wear but, she thought smugly, sent an unmistakable signal.

Alicia had pulled out all the stops, too. How someone so diminutive could manage to look so damned sophisticated escaped Suze. It might've been the three-inch wedge sandals that tied around her ankles. Or the linen sundress that swirled flame red at the hem, transitioned to flamingo pink at the waist, and ended in black and white polka dots at the bodice. The oversize white Jackie O sunglasses added another, undeniably chic touch.

Fending off the ecstatic Doofus with one hand, Alicia slid the sunglasses down her nose with the other. Since her eyes were pretty much level with Suze's boobs, they couldn't miss the red unit patch.

"Is that your unit?"

"The 56th Fighter Wing," Suze confirmed.

With some effort, she managed to refrain from shooting the traitor now slavishly twining himself around the other woman's legs an evil glance.

"It dates back to 1947, when it was part of SAC and provided defense of our northern tier. Now we're part of Air Education and Training Command and are the initial training base for F-35 aircrews."

"I have no clue what any of that means," Alicia admitted with one of her tinkling laughs, "but it sounds pretty impressive to a small-town Oklahoma girl. Oh, I meant to *this* small-town Oklahoma girl."

Your choice, Suze wanted to say. Nobly, she refrained. "Would you like something to drink? I can make a fresh pot of coffee. Or there's water and iced tea in the fridge."

"Iced tea would be good."

Once in the kitchen, the Realtor plopped her Kate Spade bag and leather briefcase on the counter. She accepted the tea and helped herself to a packet of sweetener before trying to bridge the gap between personal and professional.

"Look, I know this is as awkward for you as it is for me…"

"Not quite," Suze drawled.

She was tempted, *really* tempted, to flash her new diamond band but surprised both herself and her guest with an apology.

"Sorry, Alicia. I didn't mean to sound so catty."

"Well…"

"And while we're at it, I guess I should say I'm sorry we never clicked in school."

Alicia's delicately feathered brows soared. After a startled moment, she acknowledged their long-standing rift with a rueful smile.

"Me, too, although we both know the reason why. I fell for Gabe, like, two days after my family moved to Cedar Creek. He was such a hottie and so sweet to the new girl in school. I guess I wasn't exactly subtle about it."

"Subtle, no. Persistent, yes."

"Lot of good it did me." She folded her elbows on the briefcase and propped her chin in her hands. "I won't lie to you, Suzanne. When you and Gabe divorced, I went after him with every weapon in my arsenal. Almost succeeded in nailing him, too."

"I know. He told me."

"He should've been such easy pickings. He was so lonely when you two separated."

He wasn't the only one. Suze cringed inside, wondering if Gabe had told Alicia that his wife had turned to another man for comfort.

No. He wouldn't do that. The hurt would've been too deep, too personal. Still, she had to take a quick swallow as Alicia surveyed the kitchen with a proprietary eye.

"Did he tell you I started my campaign by helping him with the renovations?"

"He seems to have neglected to mention that."

"You may be the construction engineer, but my degree's in interior design. I suggested these smooth-planed planks for the floor and the river stone for the fireplace. Gabe liked the idea of incorporating the key elements of Cedar Creek's environment."

Since Suze was once again wearing his ring, she could afford to be generous. "I like it, too, Alicia. I especially love all the windows and skylights. They bring the outside in. You did an amazing job."

"I did, didn't I?" Looking smug, the Realtor unclipped her briefcase. "You'll have to tell Dave Forrester next time you see him. I've been pestering him to turn me loose in that mausoleum he built out in Stony Brook Estates."

"I didn't know he'd built out there."

"Six-thousand square feet's worth. I'm going to meet him there at noon, so we'd better get to work."

Once she had her iPad in hand, flighty, flirty Alicia transformed into SuperRealtor. She clicked picture after picture, added dimensions, laid on the superlatives.

"You know," she said as Suze and Doofus walked her to the front door, "Gabe could make twice what he put into the house if he decided to sell instead of rent."

"Renting is good for now. But don't offer more than a year's lease. We're not sure where we'll be after the baby's born."

"So the rumor's true?" Alicia's gaze dive-bombed to Suze's middle, zinged up again. "You're pregnant?"

Suze didn't bother to ask where she'd heard the rumor. With three ecstatic grandparents-to-be and six siblings-in-law, some version of the news was bound to leak.

"It's true."

Alicia's smile didn't convey quite its usual brilliance, but her congratulations were heartfelt. "That's great, Suzanne. I'm happy for you and Gabe. Honestly. But renting for just one year with no option to extend may restrict your customer base."

"We'll take that chance."

"Okay. Well…" She held out a hand. "Congratulations again. I sincerely hope you and Gabe make it work this time."

"That's what she said?" Suze's mom asked an hour later. "She hoped you two would make it work *this* time?"

They were in the kitchen, preparing their contribution to the family picnic to come later that afternoon. Mary sprinkled bright red paprika over two trays of deviled eggs while Suze turned the last of the sizzling chicken in the cast-iron frying pan.

"That's what she said."

"If I didn't believe in saying no evil," her mother muttered with a determined shake of the paprika container, "I'd have a name for that woman. I probably shouldn't tell you this but…well…" Another vigorous shake. "Someone told Kathy she stripped naked and went skinny-dipping in the creek out behind Gabe's house. Just her bad luck he'd gone over to Ok-City and didn't get back until she was shriveled up like a…"

"Mom! That's enough paprika. We'd better shove this stuff in the fridge and get downtown. The parade starts in twenty minutes."

Her mother abandoned the spice and dusted her hands on her navy-blue slacks. She'd topped them with a round-necked red T-shirt, and, to her daughter's delight, she'd also gone in for a new do. The turquoise tips were gone. Her chin-length bob now sported streaks of red and blue amid the snowy white.

Given the limited wardrobe Suze had brought with

her, she opted to go with white jeans and her royal blue Warrior Mom T-shirt. If Alicia had heard a rumor about the baby, it had to be all over town anyway.

"Are you going to ride in the parade with Gabe?" her mother wanted to know.

"He's participating as mayor. I don't think…"

"Well, I do! You're the mayor's wife. You should be there with him."

She might've still held out if Gabe hadn't called her just as she and her folks joined the herd of excited kids and indulgent parents streaming toward downtown.

"Where are you?"

"On 5th, about to turn onto Main."

"Cut across to 3rd. And hurry. We're in the third slot, right behind the VFW color guard and Colonel Amistad's car."

He hung up before she could ask him whether his crew had plugged the water main. Yielding to the combined pressure of her husband and her parents, Suze cut through the alley between the pharmacy and Dottie's Antiques & Collectibles.

She found Gabe standing beside a vintage convertible with a magnetic placard on each door identifying the passenger as Cedar Creek's mayor. She guessed he'd come straight from the leak site. His jeans were wet from the knee down, no doubt from hosing off layers of mud, but he must've swung by his office to grab a sport coat.

He was standing next to a uniformed Air Force officer who had racks of ribbons climbing almost all the way up to his shoulder. Although Suze hadn't met Colonel George Amistad before, she knew him by reputation. He'd risen through the ranks from wrench bender to officer candidate to hotshot pilot to commander of the Air National Guard unit that shared a runway with Will Rogers Airport.

His wife accompanied him. The petite, blue-eyed blonde was a direct descendent of the Choctaw chief who'd led his tribe over the Trail of Tears. The Amistads lived on the south side of Oklahoma City but given Cedar Creek's close proximity to the FAA and Will Rogers Airport, Gabe interacted with the colonel frequently on community matters and had asked him to act as grand marshal of the parade this year.

Suze's salute was automatic, unthinking, a junior officer's tribute to an officer, a gentleman and a hero. He returned it with the same courtesy.

"I read about your Bronze Star, Captain Hall. Sounded like you took some heat down range."

"Just a little, sir."

"Proud of you."

"Thank you."

"Proud of your hubby, too." He clapped a hand on Gabe's shoulder. "I hate that the Air Force lost someone with his smarts, but he's done a great job as mayor. Sure would like to see him run for national office before I die. Senator Hall has a ring to it, don't you think?"

His comment was so close to Suze's previous thoughts that she blinked. "Yes, sir."

"How about you come see me tomorrow. You and Gabe? We're the first Guard unit to bed down the new MC-12. I think you'll both be interested in its capabilities."

They'd planned to get serious about packing tomorrow but both recognized a politely veiled order when they heard one.

"We can do that," Gabe confirmed.

"Good. Make it around ten. We can…"

A shrill, ear-piercing screech made them all wince. It emanated from the toy whistle blown by a sweating Dr. Peterman. The chubby, round-faced dentist wind-milled his arms at the various lead elements.

"Showtime, everyone!"

The band formed into neat lines. The volunteer fire-fighters jumped aboard their pumper. The still incred-ibly hard-bodied Joanna Hicks adjusted her rhinestone crown, twitched her Mrs. Oklahoma sash into place and ascended to the throne mounted on the bunting-draped trailer being towed by her adoring husband. The floats and bands behind them scrambled into position.

Harried, Doc Peterman rushed over to shoo the grand marshal, the mayor and their wives to their vehicles. Suze joined her husband in the backseat of the vintage Corvette. The band launched into John Philip Souza's "The Stars and Stripes Forever." The VFW honor guard stepped out. Colonel Amistad's vehicle followed at a sedate speed. The Corvette kept a respectful distance behind him, and Cedar Creek's Fourth of July celebra-tions were officially underway.

The family picnic that followed the parade was quint-essential Small Town, America. For all Suze's youth-ful eagerness to shake off the dust of Cedar Creek and explore the world, she cherished her memories of oc-casions like this.

The Hall and Jackson clans congregated at Gabe's place so the kids and Doofus could splash in the creek. Shrieking and woofing, they frolicked under the watchful eyes of assorted grandparents, parents, aunts and older cousins.

Hot dogs and hamburgers sizzled on the grill. Foil-wrapped sweet corn steamed. Suze nuked the chicken she'd fried that morning at her mom's house while Gabe's brothers-in-law dumped ice into chests crammed with beer and soft drinks. Their wives loaded portable picnic tables with Jell-O salads, deviled eggs, potato salad, baked beans, fried okra and an assortment of chips.

A stranger surveying the mounded platters and Saran-covered bowls might doubt the feast could all be consumed at one sitting, and it wasn't. Everyone made several passes over the next few hours, however. A lively game of volleyball later in the afternoon revived appetites enough for the homemade ice cream to make an appearance to a round of applause, along with the iced watermelon and angel food cake topped with strawberries, blueberries and whipped cream.

When the sun slid behind the tree line, the tables were cleared, the kids corralled and the lawn chairs folded for easy carrying. Then the whole group traipsed the few blocks to Veterans' Memorial Park. Although it was just coming on to dusk, tiny white lights outlined the roof and posts of the newly painted Victorian bandstand. The Combined Senior Adult Choir and orchestras from the four churches in town were assembling for their traditional patriotic concert. Suze's mom abandoned the family to take her place among the sopranos, while her dad went to help with the speakers and mics.

Half the town was already in place, their lawn chairs and blankets riding the gentle slope in front of the bandstand. As Suze and Gabe and the rest of their family wove their way to a vacant spot, friends and neighbors she hadn't seen in years congratulated her and Gabe on their remarriage. Several also offered congratulations on the baby.

"The village tom-toms must've been thumping non-stop," she commented drily.

"Comes with the territory. How's this spot, gang?"

With the enthusiastic approval of the rest of the clan, Gabe helped unfold lawn chairs, then went to make sure his crews had everything in place for the fireworks.

"Be back when I can."

When he strode off, his mother crooked a finger. "Here, take this chair next to mine, Suzanne. You've been so busy, we haven't really had a chance to just sit and chat since you got home."

"I know, Violet, and I'm sorry for that."

Suze settled in the woven green-and-white chair and yielded to little Tildy's demands for a cuddle. With the toddler wide-eyed and nested comfortably in her lap, Suze surveyed choir and orchestra.

"How many of these Fourth of July concerts have you attended?" she asked her mother-in-law.

"Dan and I made about every one."

Violet lowered her eyes, her thoughts turned inward for a moment. Even after all these years, she still missed her husband. Suze remembered him as a big, bluff, generous-hearted man who loved to play dominoes with his pals from the VFW.

"We couldn't come the year Penny was in the hospital, so sick with meningitis. I had to take a pass last year, too, because of this danged hip replacement."

"You're still limping pretty badly. Did you do physical therapy?"

"Three months of it." She made a face. "Getting old is not for the faint of heart."

"So my mom and dad keep telling me."

Tildy spotted her older siblings and demanded to be set down. Her chubby legs pumping, she chased after the others under the watchful eye of her parents and aunts and uncles. Her grandmother kept an eye on her as well, before turning to her daughter-in-law.

"I'm so happy about the baby, Suzanne."

"Me, too."

She really was. Coming home had vanquished her initial doubts and fears. Coming home and falling in love with Gabe all over again.

Except…

As she and Gabe had discussed, she would be on restricted duty until after the baby was born. Then it would be another six months before she became eligible for worldwide duty again. Her unit at Luke would have to work around her during that long stretch.

She couldn't quite quash a niggling feeling of guilt at leaving her team in the lurch. And wondering just how she and Gabe would handle the separations once she was eligible to deploy again. Being apart so much had wreaked havoc on their marriage before.

He was determined this time would be different. That *they* were different. She had to believe he was right.

The orchestra began to tune up. The choirs shifted into place. Under the cover of squeaky reeds, sliding trombones and shuffling feet, Violet said softly, "I've had time to think about Gabe going back to Phoenix with you. I admit I didn't much like the idea when the two of you told me."

Suze flicked a glance at her sisters-in-law. Penny and Jill sat next to each other, their heads together as they laughed over some private joke. Kathy was adjusting her eldest daughter's headband, an elaborate affair that sported an array of blinking, bobbing, red, white and blue stars. Their husbands stood in a loose cluster, no doubt assessing the latest acquisition by Oklahoma City's pro basketball team.

"You weren't the only one who didn't like the idea."

"Yes, well, I've changed my mind. I think you're doing the right thing."

Suze felt her jaw sag. As the orchestra's only flautist trilled in the background, she stared at her mother-in-law in surprise. Smiling, Violet reached for her hand.

"Cedar Creek is your home. Your roots go bedrock deep. So do Gabe's. But this town may be filled with too many memories for you both, and too many people who want a piece of your lives. So it could be that you need to build a new life together, just you and Gabe and the baby. Then, when you're ready, come home again."

Before Suze could reply, the conductor rapped his baton on his music stand and called for quiet. The talk and laughter buzzed down, the conductor turned back to face his silver-haired performers and the concert kicked off with "This Land Is Your Land," a much-loved favorite by Oklahoma's own Woody Guthrie.

Suze joined in the singing but Violet's comments kept circling in her head. They were still there when Gabe rejoined the group.

"Fireworks all set to go?" his mother asked.

"All set. It's going to be a heck of a show."

He repeated the same promise when he was called to the stage. He also thanked the orchestra, the choirs and the volunteers working the lighting, sound, safety and cleanup.

He stood so tall and handsome and at ease beside the podium. He used no notes while he reminded his listeners about the men and women who'd fought for and defended the country's independence. And were still fighting to defend it, he said with a deliberate glance in his wife's direction.

Suze flushed at the spontaneous applause and faces turned in her direction. Gabe waited for it to die down before emphasizing that gatherings like this were taking place all across America.

"Celebrating our fundamental freedoms with friends and family is what keeps this community and this country strong. Whatever happens in Washington, we stand together in Cedar Creek."

He stepped down to hearty applause, topped by a shout from an appreciative female constituent. "Justin Trudeau and that Macron dude got nothing on you, Mayor! You just keep on doin' what you're doin'."

Hoots and laughter followed him back to his seat. As the choir began a stirring medley, Suze leaned closer. "You must not have told anyone about moving to Arizona. The jungle drums would've been working overtime."

"I gave Joanna Hicks a heads-up but asked her to keep it quiet until after the Fourth. I'll present my formal resignation at the town council meeting tomorrow afternoon. Tonight is just for having fun, not saying goodbye."

Despite his easy slouch, Gabe kept his eyes on his watch as he counted down to the fireworks display. The town's pumper and crew were parked right at the edge of the dirt lot where the contractor providing the pyrotechnic display had set up. His fellow volunteer firefighters were monitoring their phones, prepared to respond instantly. An ambulance from the regional hospital was five minutes away.

When tragedy struck, however, it didn't happen at the carefully controlled site. The first indication was a loud *ka-boom* that jerked everyone around. The second was a wild burst of fireworks gyrating like corkscrews through the sky to the east. Gabe was already shoving out of his chair when his phone shrilled. He answered, then took off at a run.

"Stoney Brook Estates," he threw over his shoulder. "Chuck Osborne's place. Be back when I can."

Suzanne was only a half-step behind him. She knew the Emergency Action Checklist for On-Scene Commanders backward and forward. If nothing else, she could help at the command center, work the communications or coordinate relief efforts. Whatever Gabe or his on-scene commander needed.

## *Chapter Nine*

Gabe, the fire chief and the medical examiner pieced the sequence of events together after the fact. Tragically, the Osborne fire had resulted from one of those freak accidents people read about but never believe could really happen.

Chuck Osborne and his two young sons had decided to hold their own Independence Day celebration. In preparation, Chuck had almost bought out one of the fireworks tents that sprouted up like mushrooms throughout Oklahoma in late June. He and the boys had shot off parts of their cache the previous couple of nights but saved the biggest and best for the Fourth.

Then Chuck, a savvy avionics systems instructor at FAA who damned well should've known better, leaned over to light the fuse of a rocket mounted on a launcher stuck in the ground. The rocket exploded prematurely and rammed straight into his chest. The force of the hit had stopped his heart and fiery sparks set his shirt alight.

One of his frantic sons had tried to douse the fire by rolling him in the dirt but the boy was too young and his dad was too heavy to roll. The other son raced for the garden hose. By the time he'd tugged the hose as far as it would reach and arced a stream of water at his father, flames were devouring the tinder-dry grass around him.

When Gabe and Suze arrived, it was a scene right out of their worst nightmares. Thick black smoke blotted out the evening sky. Flames formed a seemingly impenetrable wall stretching from the Osbornes' home to the fields behind it. The blazing backdrop illuminated the two- and three-hundred-thousand-dollar homes scattered at wide intervals through the development.

The fire chief gave Gabe a quick sit rep. "Chuck Osborne's dead. His son said a rocket augered into his chest and exploded. Wife says she saw his body enveloped in flames. The boys suffered burns, don't know how bad yet. Donna, too. They're on their way to the regional hospital."

Gabe squinted at the roiling smoke and dancing flames. "We need help with this, chief."

"Already put out the call for aid from our surrounding communities. Mustang's pumpers and tanker are five minutes out. Yukon and OKC are responding, too."

"What about a Hot Shot cadre?"

"I've notified the Forestry Service," the chief confirmed. "They're sending a team. They'll also call in air support."

The taut reply knotted Suze's stomach. It stayed bunched as her husband pulled on the turnout gear he'd picked up at the station on their mad race out of town—bunker pants, jacket, boots, gloves and helmet with its protective visor.

Just rigging out in the scorching July night drenched him in sweat. As he strapped on his single-harness chest-radio pack, Suze had to bite back the suggestion that he should direct the effort, not put himself on the front line. Gabe might be the town's mayor, but he was also a volunteer firefighter. She knew there was no way in hell he'd keep a safe distance from those vicious flames while his fellow volunteers were battling them.

The fire chief didn't argue, either. He'd trained these men and women. Put them through hell before he certified them. And he needed every damned one on the line.

"I've sent the A team to work the Osborne house," he advised Gabe tersely. "I have two other teams clearing a firebreak between it and the Forrester place. Might save it, if the wind doesn't pick up."

Gabe was assigned to A team. Her heart in her throat, Suze watched him hurry down the road to join the group aiming a fat inch-and-a-half stream of water at the flames engulfing the Osbornes' home.

"What can I do?" she asked the chief.

His narrowed, smoke-reddened eyes cut from the fire to her. She'd known him for most of her life. More to the point, he knew her.

"Every damned TV and radio station in central Oklahoma wants an update and Hal Jorgenson, our Public Affairs officer is down with colitis. Our deputy PA's on her way. Until she gets here…"

He jerked his head toward his command vehicle.

The driver's door hung open. Suze could hear the shrill squawks and tinny requests for status from where she stood.

"You know what to tell 'em, Captain. And what *not* to tell 'em. Take care of it."

Suze took care of it until the deputy PA screeched up in a mud-spattered pickup.

"Thanks for covering for me," she panted. "You start a log?"

"Right here."

The farmer's wife skimmed the log and let out a low whistle. "Can you stay? Looks like I might need some help."

"You got it."

The two women acted as the central point of contact for news crews and concerned officials for the next two hours. They shared information on the teams that had raced to the scene from the mutual aid townships, relayed updates provided by the chief to include the arrival of the Hot Shot team and an incident commander specially trained to combat wildfires, and coordinated with Will Rogers World Airport tower to keep the air space clear for the tanker that flew in to drop fire retardant.

Suze was guzzling down bottled water when a Mustang City crew radioed a terse report.

"The heat got to our bulldozer operator. We're retreating to our fallback position to cool him down."

The water bottle crunched and crinkled in her fist. The Mustang crew had been plowing up cedars to keep the fire from jumping the creek toward the west boundary of the development. The flames had to be getting perilously close to their position. If the cedars ignited, the fire could whip along the entire creek, maybe even snake though town.

While the deputy PA briefed the chief, the urgency of the situation ripped at Suze. One dozer could clear more brush and vegetation in ten minutes than a full crew hacking and axing for several hours. She wasn't a trained firefighter but she could operate a variety of heavy equipment, including some earth movers.

Years of training and experience warred in her mind with the possible risks to her baby. She'd already exposed her unborn child to one potentially toxic situation during cleanup of the fuel spill. Did she dare risk exposing it to another?

The escalating situation forced her choice. One life had already been lost. Other folks stood to lose all they owned. She couldn't stand by and just watch.

"I can drive a dozer," she told the chief. "I might be able to help."

He didn't waste time arguing. "Go!"

Spinning, she headed for Ole Blue. Three miles and a racketing drive over unpaved roads later, she screeched to a halt at the Mustang crew's fallback position.

Sweat drenched and smoke stained, they'd propped their woozy dozer operator against a rear tire of the flatbed trailer that had transported his machinery. They'd removed his protective gear and had hosed him down and were now waiting for his body temp to lower enough for him to take in some liquid.

"I'm Suzanne Hall," she told the team leader. "Captain Suzanne Hall. I command an Air Force Prime BEEF crew and have hands-on experience operating a bulldozer."

The firefighter looked her up and down. What he saw obviously didn't reassure him but before he could question her qualifications the man beside him widened his red-rimmed eyes.

"Hey! Aren't you the captain from Cedar Creek who got the Bronze Star?"

"That's me."

"I read about her in the paper, Mike. If she says she can operate a dozer, I believe her."

She understood the team leader's skepticism even as she yanked on the dozer operator's gear. Firefighting bulldozer drivers were a rare breed. She'd read one report indicating that of the more than fourteen hundred firefighters in Orange County, California, only two were bulldozer operators. The Mustang fire department was damned lucky to have a volunteer operator. Even luckier that he happened to own a construction company and could haul in crawlers and backhoes in a crisis like this.

Although officers in charge of Prime BEEF teams weren't expected to get down in the trenches, Suze had decided early in her career to acquire at least a basic familiarity with her team members' unique skill sets. Consequently, she'd learned the intricacies of emergency airfield lighting systems, had wrestled with mobile arresting barriers, and had a working knowledge of HVAC and sanitary systems.

She'd also learned to operate various items of heavy equipment. The dump trucks were a breeze. The graders and backhoes took a little practice. Surprisingly, the dozers with their hydrostatic transmissions and GPS machine controls were also relatively easy to operate. Still, her team had held their collective breath when she'd dropped the blade and attacked a heavily damaged runway during a deployment at a remote base in Iraq—then whooped when she plowed up an entire section of cratered concrete in the first pass.

She felt that same grim determination now. She was fierce. Focused. Straining to hear every word gasped out by the heat-stricken dozer operator.

"Come at the bank…from an angle. Watch for wash-outs and cuts. Don't let 'er tip…into the creek."

"Got it."

"Make sure…you have an escape plan. If the…fire burns over you, unfurl the curtains and…plow through to the black."

The thick, reflective curtains would cover the dozer's window and provide a protective cocoon if the flames surrounded it. But even with the shield down and the built-in air-conditioning blasting, she knew temperatures inside the cab could still reach upwards of a hundred and seventy degrees. The black, she guessed, was the charred land behind the fire line.

As she started for the dozer parked down at the creek, the team leader was still dubious. "You sure you know what you're doing, Captain?"

"Guess we'll both find out quick enough."

As she approached the crawler, the fire-fed heat sucked the air from her lungs. Panting, she swung into the cab and slammed the door. She kept one foot braced against the floor and the other on the deceleration pedal as she hit the starter. The hundred-and-fifty horsepower engine rumbled under her and the air gushing through the AC vents went from hot and acrid to cool and acrid. Keeping her hands on the throttle, she squinted at the tree-lined bank ahead.

Smoke, dust and darkness threatened to obscure her visibility. The fire retardant dropped by the tankers had splattered the cab's windows with red splotches. Jaw locked, she raised the blade, dropped it again and dug it into the red Oklahoma dirt at a shallow angle. With grim determination, she throttled forward.

The twisted, stunted cedars lining the bank went down like dominoes. Their trunks crunched under the blade. Branches whipped at the crawler's sides. Perched eight feet above the fallen trees, Swish rolled along at a blinding five miles an hour while doing her damnedest to keep the tractor from tipping into the creek. Her insides squeezed when the left tread slipped and seemed to lose traction. The cab swayed, but she got it righted and kept plowing.

It was after midnight before the more than two hundred firefighters who'd responded finally tamed the beast. It had consumed over a thousand acres, most of them the open fields that stretched from Cedar Creek toward the FAA center a dozen miles to the east. The Osbornes' home was a total loss. Dave Forrester's newly constructed mansion had sustained some smoke and water damage and would need extensive repair.

Gabe hadn't seen his wife since they'd parted some five hours ago, but he'd heard via the chief that she'd joined forces with a crew from Mustang. He'd connected with her once by phone to make sure she was okay. He could tell her adrenaline was still pumping as she described the firebreak they'd established. But when she called him to let him know the Mustang crew had shut down operations, he could hear the weariness in her voice.

But that was Suze. The woman gave 200 percent to every task, every challenge. It was what made her so good at her job. And what put her squarely in line to shoot up the ranks.

Guilt nagged at him for forcing her to choose between him and her career three years ago. He could only swear a silent oath that they would do better this time around.

"Where are you now?" he asked her.

"On my way back to the command center."

"We've got things under control here. Go home. Take a cool shower. Crash. I'll get a ride home from the chief."

"Have you heard how Mrs. Osborne and the boys are doing?"

"The youngest, Danny, is in bad shape. He's been evacuated to the burn center at Integris Hospital in OKC. Donna and the oldest weren't burned as badly, but they're both pretty traumatized."

"I feel so, so sorry for them."

"Yeah, me, too. Go home," he repeated, scrubbing the heel of his hand across his chin. "Get some sleep. I'll try not to let Doofus wake you when I roll in."

Suze didn't argue. She was hot, sweat-grimed and totally whipped. She managed a smile for Doofus's ecstatic greeting and hung loose on the back patio while he made his usual mad dash around the yard, watering everything that caught his fancy.

His duty done, he bounded up the stairs ahead of her and leaped onto the bed. She didn't have the energy or the inclination to order him off. Leaving him in gleeful possession, she peeled off her clothes and left a trail all the way to the shower.

The pelting water revived her enough to shampoo her hair. That helped get most of the grime out from under her nails. Still, toweling the thick mane dry just about sucked out her the last of her energy. Head bent, towel still working, she padded back to the bedroom.

Suddenly, she stopped dead. Her discarded jeans lay in a heap, her panties next to them. The dark blotch staining the panties started her heart hammering in her chest.

"Oh, God!" Her fists tightened on the towel ends. Her legs went rubbery. "OhGod, ohGod, ohGod."

Doofus jerked up his head. His ears pricked forward, and he gave a low whine when Suze dropped to one knee. He was beside her, nosing her arm, when she snatched up the panties. She shoved him away and sat back on her heels.

The stain was dry. Rust colored. She stared at it for what felt like ten lifetimes, then shoved to her feet and rushed downstairs. With Doofus clicking at her heels, she cut straight for the laptop on Gabe's desk. He'd shared the password so it took her only a few seconds to power up, log on, and Google *pregnancy, spotting.* She read at least a dozen articles before her heart stopped hammering.

"Okay," she told the anxious hound who'd plopped his head onto her thigh. "Okay. It's not uncommon in the first few weeks. As long as the blood isn't bright red and I didn't experience any cramps, we don't need to worry."

She hadn't cramped. Had she?

Her pulse skittered. With the bulldozer's engine rumbling under her and the blade chewing up cypress after cypress and her adrenaline pumping a gallon a minute, would she have felt a cramp if she'd had one?

She considered calling her mother. Or Gabe's mother. As late as it was, she ruled them out and called his oldest sister, instead. Kathy had more than six years as a neonatal intensive care nurse under her belt. Suze hated to wake her on one of her rare nights off but knew she could trust her judgment.

Her voice clogged with sleep, Kathy demanded an update on the fire first, then echoed the articles her sister-in-law had pulled up. "Yeah, it's not unusual. I spotted with two of my kids. I wouldn't worry about it, unless it continues or you start cramping."

Reassured, Suze thanked her and disconnected. For her own peace of mind, though, she walked the floor for another twenty minutes. Doofus watched every turn and foray she made to the bathroom to check for additional spotting. When none appeared, she fell into bed, too relieved and exhausted to stay awake for Gabe's return.

Gabe and the chief swung by the station to clean and stash their protective gear before heading home. Half the company had already stood down but a team would remain on-site to watch for flare-ups. They would also secure the scene for reps from the Oklahoma State Fire Marshall's office, which was charged with investigating any fire involving loss of life and/or property damage above a certain level.

Gabe had the chief drop him off at the end of the drive, hoping he could walk up to the house and slip inside before Doofus went nuts. The plan almost worked. He got through the front door and was halfway up the stairs before the hound launched into full alert mode.

The sudden, startled barking rattled the windows. His claws scrabbled on the wood floor. And when he appeared at the top of the stairs, the acrid stink of smoke clinging to the shadowy figure coming up apparently confused the heck out of him.

"Yeah, it's me."

Reassured by the sound of his human's voice, Doofus went from confused to ecstatic. He danced beside Gabe as he went into the bedroom and dropped a kiss on Suze's cheek.

"Whattimeizzit?"

"Coming up on 3:00 a.m. Go back to sleep. I'll join you shortly."

"Shortly" stretched out for a good twenty minutes. His back against the shower tiles, he lifted his face and tried to let the lukewarm stream wash away some of the horror of the night.

But try as he might, he couldn't shut down the chaotic sounds and sights that kalidescoped through his mind. The flames leaping into the night sky. The charred bodies. The utter weariness in Suze's voice when he'd talked to her.

Christ! The woman was incredible. She'd jumped aboard a bulldozer and plunged into a raging fire. Yet now, with the adrenaline drained out of him, a nasty little niggle of doubt picked at the edges of his weariness.

Flattening a palm against the tile, Gabe let the water pound his head and shoulder. He'd told Suze he would support her. That he would jettison the job and the home that he loved to move to Phoenix. That once the baby was born, they would work out their future together, one day at a time.

And as long as she wore an Air Force uniform, the

odds were the future would include more toxic spills. More aircraft accidents and explosions and raging fires. More deployments to dangerous forward locations.

Could he handle saying goodbye to her again? Stand by while she packed her go-kit, kissed him and the baby, and left?

He'd convinced her he could. Convinced himself he could. But now, with the horror of the night still smoldering in his mind, Gabe couldn't help wonder if he was deluding himself.

His mind as tired as his body, he pried his shoulder blades from the wall, shampooed, soaped down, dried off and slid between the sheets. Suze mumbled something that sounded distinctly grumpy and bucked her butt against his hip. Gabe rolled onto his side and spooned her body with his.

The feel of her, the scent of her, his provided an instant counter to his doubts. He settled her closer and repeated what he suspected might become his personal mantra. The months and years ahead wouldn't be easy. For him, or for her. But this time they'd make it, dammit. They would!

He fell asleep with that fierce vow echoing in his mind and his wife in his arms.

His side of the bed was empty when Suze woke the next morning. She shuffled to the bathroom, still groggy. The sight of the panties she'd rinsed out last night draped over the side of the tub brought her fear crashing back. She didn't draw a whole breath until she made sure she hadn't spotted again during the night.

Relieved, she followed the scent of coffee to the kitchen. A note propped on the counter informed her that Gabe had an early morning meeting with the state fire inspectors. It also reminded her of the ten o'clock meeting with Colonel Amistad. Gabe would have to cancel but encouraged her to make the meeting.

She stood at the counter, undecided. The breakfast table was covered with empty packing boxes and wrapping paper. So was the dining table. Since Alicia was sure she could rent the house furnished, they'd decided to leave the big stuff and basic necessities like dishes and pots and pans. But they still needed to pack the personal items that Gabe wanted to put in storage.

Suze's gaze swept the empty boxes. What the hell. Both she and Gabe had packed up and moved often enough before. Still plenty of time left.

Since she'd run through the limited wardrobe she'd brought with her, she called the sister-in-law nearest to her size.

"Penny, I need to borrow something suitable for a meeting with Colonel Amistad."

"Who?"

"He was Grand Marshal of the parade."

"If you say so. Come on over. *Mi* closet *es su* closet."

Twenty minutes later, Suze left her sister-in-law's house wearing a pair of black slacks and a sleeveless, amber-colored linen tunic. Since her feet were two sizes larger than Penny's, she slipped into the sling-backs she'd bought for the wedding and belted the tunic with the matching, cream-colored belt.

She clipped her hair up as a concession to the heat but couldn't bring herself to put up the T-bird's top. As a result, she had to make herself presentable again when she pulled into a visitor's slot outside the headquarters of the 137th Special Operations Wing. She sat in the vicious sun, raking her fingers through her hair, twisting it up again, while her gaze roamed the buildings and hangars visible from where she'd parked.

She had a feeling she knew what had prompted this invitation to meet with the 137th commander. He knew her background. Knew, too, that his unit could make use of her training and hard learned experience.

She'd taken a few minutes to Google the 137th before leaving for her meeting with its commander. The wing's long and distinguished history stretched back to 1947, when it began life as a fighter group flying the F-51 Mustang.

Now the 137th was transitioning to a new platform. Smaller, sleeker and crammed with the world's most sophisticated avionics, communications and surveillance equipment. Suze could see several of the MC-12 Liberties parked on the apron. From where she was standing they looked like corporate turboprops, which is precisely how the modified Hawker Beechcraft Super Kings had begun life. She couldn't wait to get an up close and personal tour. When she was ushered into the colonel's office, however, Amistad suggested a chat before he had one of the MC-12 pilots show off his baby.

"I'm sorry Gabe couldn't make it," he said when they'd settled at the small round table against a wall that displayed all the unit awards the wing had won. "I understand why, though. Our fire crews didn't return to base until well past midnight. I image Cedar Creek's mayor stayed on scene for hours after that."

"He did, and he said to tell you how much he appreciated your engines responding as quickly as they did. He'll send an official thank-you as soon as he can."

"No problem. And actually, you're the one I really wanted to talk to this morning."

At her questioning look, he flicked a glance at her wedding band. "You know how the rumor mill works. Word is, now that you and Gabe are back together he's moving to Phoenix with you."

"The rumor mill has it right." She hesitated, then filled in the rest of the blanks. "We're also going to have a baby."

"I heard that, too. Not that it makes any difference for what I'd like to propose."

She'd guessed what was coming before he laid the offer on the table.

"Our civil engineering chief plans to retire next year. He's an Air Reserve Technician, with more than thirty years under his belt."

Suze's knowledge of Air National Guard operations was sketchy but she understood that an ART combined two worlds. As a civilian, an ART worked the same job in the same place, generally keeping fairly normal duty hours, until retirement.

At the same time, ARTs were members of the Air Force Reserve Command. As such, they wore their uniforms and rank. And like all members of the Guard and Reserve, they were subject to mobilization and deployment.

"The position is competitive," Amistad confirmed, "so we'll advertise it Air Force–wide. But with your background and experience, you'd have a real shot at it."

When she started to reply, he held up a palm.

"You might not deploy as often as you do now, but I can't make any promises. Last year we sent various elements of the wing to a half-dozen hot spots around the world. The difference is, you'll home base here, in Oklahoma City, between deployments."

Suze's first thought was that this could be the best solution for both her and the Air Force. If she requested separation due to pregnancy, her unit at Luke could fill her vacancy. No work-arounds, no tagging someone else to deploy in her place.

Separation due to pregnancy would also allow her the time and the leisure to experience the full spectrum of motherhood. A time, her sisters-in-law warned, stretched from gestation to delivery to that scary postpartum period that would have her swinging from "Isn't the baby the most precious thing you ever saw" to "I need out of this freakin' house *now*!"

And, as the Colonel had stressed, she would home base here, in Oklahoma, instead of moving from assignment to assignment and base to base for the next thirteen or fourteen years. And that kind of stability meant Gabe could explore higher public office, as everyone seemed think he should.

Balancing all the potential positives was the prospect of working the same job in the same place for the next twenty or thirty years. She'd joined the military in the first place for the travel and excitement and adventure it offered. She loved the challenges and the fact that every transfer, every assignment meant new challenges, new adventures.

Except…she had to think of more than just herself now. And having a baby would certainly offer all kinds of challenges and adventures.

"I don't want an answer now, Captain. Think about it. Talk it over with Gabe. Get back to me when you're ready. And in the meantime…" He pushed away from the table. "How about an up close and personal tour of the MC-12 Liberty?"

Her escort was standing by. Like many Air National Guard pilots, Captain Marv Westbrook was older and more experienced than most of his active duty counterparts. He was also just back from the ten-nation NATO operation to retake Mosul.

"Flying so low and slow got a little hairy at times," he admitted in what Suze knew was a monumental understatement, "but we provided real-time intelligence, surveillance and recon to the coalition forces. You'll be impressed as hell when you see the comm and sensors packed into the Liberty."

She certainly was. She was even more impressed when Marv wrapped up his part of the tour and turned her over to the 137th's Chief of Civil Engineering. For the next hour she happily immersed herself in the world of rapid runway repair, explosive ordnance disposal and emergency humanitarian relief projects.

Seriously impressed by the 137th's operation, Suze said goodbye and made her way back to the T-bird. She'd put up a protective windshield screen but still eased onto the hot leather of the driver's seat *very* carefully. It took some maneuvering to keep the backs of her arms from making contact with the hot leather but she keyed the ignition and soon had the AC blasting.

She was still parked and waiting for the steering wheel to cool enough to wrap her palms around when her cell phone chimed. Caller ID showed "unknown caller" but the area code was local. Thinking it might be someone she'd just talked to at the 137th, she answered.

"Captain Hall."

"Hey, Suzanne. It's Dave."

She went blank for a moment before connecting the voice to her former classmate, Freckle-faced Forrester. "Hi, Dave."

"I got your mobile number from Gabe. Hope you don't mind."

"'Course not."

"I called him to let him know I'm on my way home and will bring a damage assessor out to check out the house this afternoon."

"Be prepared," she warned. "From what I could see, it looked pretty bad."

"That's what I heard. Listen, I heard you've got a meeting with Colonel Amistad. Sure wish you'd come talk to me before you sign on with the Guard. Like I told you, I could..."

"What makes you think I'm joining the Guard?"

"Hey, this boy ain't as stupid as he looks. First, Alicia tells me you're renting out the house but restricting it to a short-term lease. Then Gabe lets drop that you drove over to talk to Colonel Amistad despite the wild night I know you both had. So I figure it's about something pressing and made a few calls."

She barely heard his eager prattle. Her mind was still wondering if Gabe had known the Colonel wanted to recruit her.

"And speaking of wild nights... I heard what you did, Suzanne. Climbing aboard that dozer was pretty slick. And exactly why I want you working for me. I'm telling you, girl, the oil and gas business has done a one-eighty since the slump a few years ago. You could make four, five times what you're making now."

She shook herself out of her whirling thoughts. She

didn't bother to tell Forrester it wasn't about the money. For her *or* for most of the men and women she served with. Hell, many of the junior enlisted troops in her squadron qualified for food stamps.

"Sorry, Dave," she replied. "Not interested."

"Just think about it. Talk it over with Gabe."

Which was exactly the same advice Colonel Amistad had offered.

Feeling as though she was being yanked in a dozen different directions, Suze put the convertible in gear. To her disgust, she'd barely reached the front gates before her bladder reminded her that she'd once again downed too much coffee. Her stomach chimed in to suggest that a bacon cheeseburger wouldn't be out of order. Yielding to their urgent demands, she pulled into a conveniently located Braum's just a short distance from the base.

She hit the ladies' room first. Mere seconds later, the dark stain in her underwear sent her running out of the fast food restaurant. Big, sprawling Tinker Air Force Base to the east of Oklahoma City maintained a fully staffed medical clinic. But Tinker was a good thirty minutes away.

Shoving the T-bird into gear, she headed for the new healthplex closer to home.

## Chapter Ten

Gabe got the text while he and the fire chief still had their heads together with the state inspectors. He'd put his phone on vibrate so as not to interrupt their discussions and had let several calls go to voice mail. Then *Call me. Now!* popped up on his screen.

"'Scuse me, I need to take this." Frowning, he cut away from the others and stabbed Suze's speed dial number. "What's up?"

"I'm at the ER at the healthplex. I had some vaginal bleeding."

"Are you okay?"

"Mostly."

"The baby?"

"I'm… I'm not sure. They're going to run some tests."

"I'm on my way."

He made a quick excuse to the others and hit Ole Blue on the run.

The healthplex was only minutes away, thank God. Yet the drive seemed to take a lifetime. Gabe's stomach churned with every hiss of the wheels on the pavement. All their hopes, all their newly devised plans, had centered on the unexpected, unanticipated, miraculous result of their night together in Phoenix.

If Suze lost the baby...

If they didn't have the child to help stitch their marriage back together...

Jaw locked, knuckles bone white where he gripped the steering wheel, Gabe tore into the hospital parking lot.

Opened just a few years ago, the ultramodern facility looked and felt more like a gleaming hotel than a medical center. Even the freestanding ER offered unique lighting, soothing colors and a long, curving row of spacious exam rooms that minimized the clinical setting and maximized patient comfort.

Suze was in exam room three. She was wrapped in a hospital gown and sitting on the edge of the bed as a lab tech unsnapped the rubber tie banding her upper arm. Gabe's heart squeezed at the emotions that flashed across her face when she saw him. Relief, worry, guilt all rolled into one.

"The bleeding's stopped," she related, stretching out her free hand to take his. "The doc doesn't think it presages a miscarriage but..." She stopped, bit her lip, forced herself to continue. "But he's ordered several tests."

"This one checks your hCG," the tech confirmed as she matched the information on the label attached to blood-filled vials with the data on Suze's wristband. "That's a hormone produced by the placenta during pregnancy. Doc Terry's also ordered an ultrasound.

They're waiting to take you down now. I'll let them know you're ready."

She snapped off her gloves and tossed them in the trash, then picked up her plastic carrier with its rack of samples. Gabe had his arms around his wife before the tech was out the door.

"Oh, God." She buried her face in his shoulder. "I was so scared. Still am. I should've come in last night."

The whisper was so low and muffled Gabe wasn't sure he'd heard right. "You were bleeding last night?"

"A little, but I checked a dozen sites on the internet and…"

"Christ, Suze! You checked the internet?"

She pushed back a little. "I also called Kathy. She said spotting is fairly normal this early in a pregnancy."

"Why didn't you call me?"

"You were working the cleanup from the fire and I…"

"Are you ready, Mrs. Hall?"

A cheerful young orderly in cinnamon-colored scrubs rolled in a wheelchair. Gabe was still trying to digest the fact that Suze hadn't told him about the spotting as he walked with her down several long, spotlessly clean corridors.

The radiology tech was ready for them. "Hello, Ms. Hall. I'm Hector Alvarez. Doctor Terry's ordered an ultrasound of your abdomen. Have you had one before?"

"Yes, a few weeks ago."

"Then you know what to expect." He helped her get situated on the table, draped a sheet over her upper thighs and rolled the hospital gown up to bare her belly. "When was the last time you ate?"

"I had some instant oatmeal around eight-thirty this morning."

"Nothing since?"

"No."

"How about liquids?"

"Coffee. But it's pretty well flushed out."

"Great. We should get some clear images. Okay, here we go."

He squirted the warm gel on Suze's still-flat belly and began to move his wand. Like Suzanne, Gabe kept his focus on the screen. He'd seen copies of his various nieces' and nephews' ultrasounds stuck to his sisters' fridges with magnets. But when the tech pointed to the tiny, curled form nestled in his wife's belly, he experienced a swift, hard jab of delight.

"That's it?" he asked the tech. "That little peanut?"

"Yep, that's your baby."

Suze kept a death grip on Gabe's hand. "Is it okay?"

"The radiologist will have to review the scans but I'm not seeing anything to concern me." He worked the wand in a slow circle. Dropped it lower. Stopped and worked over the same spot again. Suze was watching the screen and missed his slight frown.

"Would you turn a little onto your left side, Ms. Hall? There. That's good."

With quick efficiency, he placed a series of electronic markers and clicked several images. Gabe leaned closer, straining to see whatever had caught the tech's attention but he'd already moved the wand to a different angle. He clicked several more images, slid the wand lower, clicked again.

"Okay, that should do it. The radiologist will review the images and zap a report to the ER toot-d-sweet. I'll just clean off that gel, and you'll be good to go."

The same cheerful orderly wheeled Suze back to

the ER. A nurse followed them into the room. "Doctor Terry's reviewing your lab results now. He'll be in as soon as he gets the radiology report."

"Good, in the meantime…" She nodded to the bathroom. "I need to go."

"No problem. Just ring if you need help."

While his wife emptied her bladder, Gabe leaned his hips against the marble windowsill. His glimpse of the ultrasound tech's small, quick frown had churned a gallon of acid in his gut. It had also kept him from letting Suze know how pissed he was that she hadn't told him about the spotting.

Granted, she'd been asleep when he got home last night. But she'd stirred enough to ask him what time it was. At the very least, she could've called him when she got up this morning.

Hell! Maybe she had. He whipped out his phone, checked the calls that had gone to voice mail and saw one from her. Cursing himself for not taking it, he listened to the short message.

Nothing about spotting. Nothing about calling Kathy. Only that she was heading for the meeting with Colonel Amistad and would see Gabe when she saw him.

There was no message from his sister, either. Jaw tight, Gabe vowed to have a discussion with Ms. Kathleen Hall Sheppard about that when he got Suze home.

But that, they discovered when the ER doc came in a few moments later, wouldn't be today. Terry looked more like a cage fighter than a physician. His shaved and shiny bald head gleamed even in the ER's subdued lighting, and his shoulders strained at the seams of his white coat. His approach matched his appearance. He was brusque and to the point, which both Gabe and Suze appreciated.

"Your tests look good, Ms. Hall. Your hCG level is elevated, as it should be. That and the ultrasound confirm your placenta hasn't abrupted."

"So I'm not losing the baby?"

"I don't think so. A lot of women experience bleeding during their pregnancies."

Suze collapsed against the raised bed back. "That's what Kathy told me. My sister-in-law," she explained. "She's a neonatal intensive care nurse here."

"Kathy Sheppard?"

"That's her."

He turned his cool, penetrating gaze on Gabe. "You're Kathy's brother? The mayor of Cedar Creek?"

"Right."

"We treated your fire victims here in the ER last night. One of the boys was transported to the burn unit at Integris. The other kid and his mom are upstairs."

"I know. I'm going up to see them before I leave."

Terry nodded and turned back to Suze. "Spotting is common, but heavy bleeding like you had this morning concerns me. Did you overexert yourself and lift something heavy in the past twenty-four hours?"

Her mouth twisted in a grimace so full of guilt that Gabe supplied the answer.

"My wife's a combat engineer. She can operate just about every piece of heavy equipment in the Air Force inventory. She helped us last night by climbing aboard a bulldozer and plowing a firebreak."

The doc's eyes narrowed. "Damn! I just made the connection. You're the Captain I read about in the paper some weeks back."

"There's something else," Suze confessed, worrying her lower lip with her teeth. "Last month, before I knew I was pregnant, my team and I responded to a fuel spill. I wore a respirator and the tests the doc at my base ran indicated no toxicity in my lungs or blood gases. But..." She chewed on her lip again, harder. "I thought you should know."

"Well..." Terry tapped his pen against the lab report. "I'm going to level with you. If you do miscarry, there's nothing we can do for you here in the ER. Nature will take its course. But if it does happen, you're in the right place. We'll watch to make sure you don't hemorrhage."

He hesitated just a second too long. The color drained from Suze's cheeks, and Gabe went still.

"There was something that popped up on the ultrasound. Nothing involving the baby," he said swiftly. "Just an anomaly we need to scope out."

"What kind of anomaly?"

"It's called a uterine mass. Could be a cyst. Could be a fibroid. Neither one is anything to worry about, but the radiologist wants another pass at it. So I'm going to admit you to the hospital and order more tests."

When Suze's eyes went wide, Gabe saw the incipient panic in their forest-green depths. Saw, too, the iron will that shut it down.

"Thanks, doc," she said, forcing a calm he knew she was far from feeling. "Run every test in the book. I'd rather err on the side of caution."

"Same here. I'll put in the admit order."

For the next few hours, Gabe had to throw up a firewall to block his chaotic thoughts from his wife. She was up to her ears in her own vicious stew of guilt and worry. He was damned if he would add to it as he accompanied her to the surgical unit, where a resident performed a needle biopsy on the uterine mass. The fact that they'd have to wait until the next day for the biopsy results only added to their combined stress.

His sister Kathy relieved some of their tension when she showed up at the healthplex several hours before she had to go on duty. She'd talked to Suze's doc before joining her brother and sister-in-law, and was quick to share what she'd learned.

"Dr. Terry's still waiting for the biopsy results," she reported after fierce hugs all around. "He's pretty convinced the mass is a uterine fibroid, though. A noncancerous growth in the muscle tissue. The technical term is leiomyoma. They're more common in older women but could certainly cause the bleeding you've experienced."

"Could it have hurt the baby?"

"I doubt it. Not at this stage. But it might crowd the fetus as it grows and presses against the mass. You should probably have it removed."

"Removed?"

"It can be done laparoscopically. Don't worry about that right now. Just relax and think happy thoughts. Which," she added with a wry smile, "is what my loving husband always advises when I'm fat and leaking and ready to take an ax to him for convincing me that we should have one more kid."

Suze laughed, which was exactly what Kathy had intended. Gabe shot her a grateful smile, then braced himself as the rest of the family followed in waves. Suze's parents. Gabe's mom, accompanied by his sister Jill. Penny and her husband and kids. Once Suze got moved to a regular room, Gabe consigned her to their collective care while he took the elevator up two floors to check on Donna Osborne and her son.

Twenty minutes later, he jabbed the down button. The brief visit had ripped him apart. Hell, the past twenty-four hours had just about shredded him. Needing some time to pull himself together, he exited the elevator and paused by the wall of windows in the family waiting area.

Despite the panorama of rolling, sun-kissed hills outside the window, his thoughts seemed to swirl in a dark vortex. He'd served in combat. Both on the ground and as the operator of an RPV armed with lethal missiles. He knew better than most that death and destruction could come at you without warning, without mercy. Now it had happened to Donna Osborne and her family.

And could happen to his *wife*!

The impact was searing. Visceral. Wrenching. The sense of having failed both Suze and the Osbornes ate at his gut. As if to counter it, the anger he'd so rigidly suppressed earlier slipped its leash.

Suze shouldn't have climbed aboard that dozer yesterday, dammit! And she should've told him about the spotting when she'd first discovered it last night. What the hell did the fact that she'd called Kathy but not him say about the state of their marriage?

The small spark of anger gathered heat. Hadn't they learned their lesson the first time around? Yet here they were, married again for all of three days, and already the lines of communication had fractured. Despite everything else going on—the wedding, the parade, the fire—she could have, *should* have called him.

He wanted to put one of his fists through the wall. He settled for jamming them in his pockets. Then he dragged in several long breaths and unlocked his jaw. This sure as hell wasn't the time or the place for *could've, should've*. His only priority right now was to be here for his wife.

Suze's parents were the last of the family to leave their daughter's spacious hospital room.

"You just rest." Mary leaned over the bed to kiss her cheek. "Hard to do in a hospital, I know, but try."

"I will."

"And you…" She wagged a stern finger at Gabe. "Call us when you know the test results. Whatever and whenever you hear."

"Will do."

When they left a silence settled over the room, broken only by the beep of a monitor from across the hall. Suze welcomed the unaccustomed quiet but roused after a few moments to tell Gabe he should go home, too.

"You need to go let Doofus out and feed him. Feed yourself, too."

"Penny's husband said he'd take care of the mutt." He dragged a chair over closer to the bed and reached for her hand. "I'll grab something at the cafeteria when they bring your supper."

Suze lay there, her fingers twined loosely with his. Despite the contact, she sensed a subtle withdrawal, as if he'd pulled into himself.

Or not. She had so much going on inside her own head she couldn't seem to get over the storm of emotions that had racked her since she hit the ladies' room at Braum's. The storm had wrung her out. She was so tired. So drained. The adrenaline that had pumped through her yesterday was a distant memory. All she had left now was a small, steely core that refused to give way to panic.

Her glance drifted to the window with its view of the parking lot below and the hills beyond. Then to Gabe. His head was bowed, his gaze on their loosely clasped hands. He was in the jeans and blue knit polo shirt he must've worn to his meeting with the state inspectors this morning. The shirt still looked trim and neat, but the face above it showed the effects of a long night and its aftermath. The white squint lines at the corners of his hazel eyes cut deep grooves. Those bracketing his mouth looked permanently etched.

He couldn't have slept more than a few hours last night. Although he slouched in the chair with his usual careless grace, his shoulders had a tired slump to them Suze couldn't remember seeing before. And even as she watched, his eyes closed for a brief moment.

"Gabe," she said quietly. "Go home."

He blinked awake instantly. "Not gonna happen, babe."

"I know you must have a stack of incident reports to review. Calls you should make. Go do what you need to do, then get some sleep. I'll be fine."

"I don't need to do anything or be anywhere or talk to anyone except you."

She sighed and let the silence spin out for another few moments.

"I guess…" She tried to keep the tremor out of her

voice but couldn't quite get there. "I guess we should talk what-ifs."

What if she lost the baby? What if their primary impetus for reconnecting disappeared? What if Gabe quit his job, resigned as mayor, moved to Arizona and hated being her military dependent when he'd previously been active duty himself. What if…?

He jerked forward, his fingers going tight on hers, and his fierce retort cut off her incipient panic. "No what-ifs. I'm not ready to play that game and you're in no condition to. Let's just take whatever happens a step at a time."

She couldn't help it. Her throat clogged. Tears burned behind her lids. Her nose got drippy. Sucking air up it, she glared at him.

"Damn these hormones! I can sure understand where Kathy was coming from."

Something flickered in his eyes at the mention of his sister, quickly came and quickly went.

"Better watch out," Suze threatened, only half in jest, "or I'll take an ax to you for turning me into this snuffling, sniffly bundle of stupid."

"You, wife, are as far from stupid as any woman I've ever known."

It sounded like a compliment. The words certainly stroked her. But was there a faint edge to his voice? Suze cocked her head, unsure.

Gabe must have sensed her puzzlement. He responded to it with a little shake of his shoulders and pushed out of his chair. "But just to be sure you don't act on any homicidal impulses…" He heeled off his shoes. "Scoot over."

"Gabe! You can't crawl in with me."

"Why not? It's not like you're hooked up to anything vital."

"True, but…"

"Scoot over."

Oh, God! She needed his arms around her. Needed his breath warm against her temple and his fierce assurance that all would be right with the world. Still snuffling, she scooted over.


She woke with a start when a white-coated physician rapped lightly on the door to her room. Blinking, she tried to guess what time it was. Late, she realized with a glance at the now-dark windows. Very late, she surmised when she squinted at the dinner sitting congealed under transparent plastic domes on her bedside tray.

She hadn't heard the food service folks deliver the dinner tray. Hadn't heard any of the nurses who must've checked on her in the hours since she'd crashed. But Gabe's murmured "We've got company," prodded her to semi-wakefulness.

"Huh?"

"We've got company."

She blinked awake to find a small, slender and obviously amused female physician observing their conjoined status. The doc's assistant stood behind her, equally amused.

Suze shifted, and Gabe vacated his half of the bed. He raked a hand through his hair, although the dark brown pelt was too short to show either the hours in the sack or any attempt to tame it.

"I'm Doctor Le," the trim young physician said as she came forward to offer Suze her hand. "I'm the hospital attending. Your case was transferred to me when you were admitted."

Her glance cut to Gabe. "And you are?"

"Her husband."

"I was certainly hoping that was the case." She shifted her attention back to Suze. "I have the results of your biopsy, Captain Hall. Dr. Terry asked me to share them with you as soon as they came. Is it okay with you if we discuss them in your husband's presence?"

Suze's arm snaked out. Gabe gripped her hand again. Harder this time.

"Yes," she said, her mouth dry.

"The biopsy confirms Dr. Terry's initial diagnosis. The mass is benign. What we call a uterine fibroid, also known as a…"

"Leiomyoma," Gabe cut in on a huff of relief.

The doc's brows rose. "Not many people are familiar with the technical term. Are you in the medical profession?"

"No, but my sister is. Kathy Sheppard. She's a nurse in the…"

"Neonatal ICU. I know Kathy. She's one of our most outstanding nurse practitioners."

Gabe and Suze exchanged glances. Apparently Kathy was well known in her sphere of operations.

"I'll tell her you said so," Gabe responded.

"And you must be the brother she's always bragging about. The mayor of…?"

"Cedar Creek."

"Right. Well…"

Suze's throat went dry, but the doc's smile worked magic on her sudden and unbelievably vicious attack of nerves.

"The mass is just large enough to press against your uterus. Your baby must have squeezed it, which is what caused the bleeding. I don't see any cause for alarm yet, but your OB/GYN needs to watch it."

"Is the baby okay?"

"Looks fine. I'll make sure you get copies of the lab report to take to your OB. Is he or she local?"

"No. I'm active duty, stationed at Luke Air Force Base in Arizona."

"A hard copy it is, then. In the meantime…" Her smile kicked up another notch. "Just relax and go back to whatever you were doing. We'll keep an eye on you tonight, Ms. Hall, but we'll probably send you home tomorrow."

When the door swished shut behind her and her PA, Suze collapsed against the pillows. To her profound disgust, a new rush of tears burned her lids.

"This is ridiculous." Thoroughly irritated, she scrubbed the back of her hand across her eyes. "How the heck am I supposed to command the respect of my troops if I go all female and weepy at the drop of a hat?"

"Jeez! We just got terrific news. You're entitled to go all weepy." Gabe gave a rueful laugh. "I'm a little soggy myself."

He was!

Biting her lip, Suze tried to remember another time when her husband's emotions had been pared down to the nub. He hadn't cried when his dad died, she recalled. Not in front of her, anyway. His mom and sisters had gone through several boxes of Kleenex at the funeral but Gabe had sat like a stone.

And he'd acted anything but maudlin at their wedding. Their first wedding, she amended. *Her* folks had shredded the Kleenex that time, but Gabe had grinned through the entire ceremony. Which made the way he dropped his chin to his chest and stared at the floor for several stark moments all the more poignant.

"Gabe," she said quietly. "Go home now. Fix something to eat, then crash. One of us, at least, should get a good night's rest."

He resisted but eventually yielded. Before leaving, though, he called her folks to share the biopsy results. Relieved and happy, they promised to swing by first thing in the morning. Suze tried to dissuade them but they silenced her protest with a promise of homemade cinnamon-raisin rolls.

"I'll be here for that, too," Gabe said with smile as he bent to kiss her goodbye. "See you in the morning."

"Let's just hope it's considerably less eventful than today's."

She was thinking of all that had happened in the space of twelve hours when she remembered the call from Dave Forrester.

"Gabe?"

She caught him halfway to the door. He turned, a question in his tired eyes.

"Yeah?"

"Did you know Colonel Amistad wanted to talk to me about a civil engineering vacancy coming up at the 137th?"

"He mentioned something about a vacancy at the parade. I assumed that was part of the reason he invited us to meet with him."

"You didn't tell me that."

"Didn't I?"

He looked at her with an expression she couldn't quite interpret, then rolled his shoulders.

"Sorry 'bout that. Guess we both need to work on our communication skills. See you in the morning."

## Chapter Eleven

Once visiting hours were over, the hospital entered that twilight world of dimmed lights and hushed voices where even the night crew's rubber-soled shoes sounded like bats squeaking in the corridors.

Kathy came by when her shift ended. She'd already tapped the nurses on Suze's floor for the biopsy results and endorsed Dr. Le's recommendation that her sister-in-law follow up with her OB when she got back to Arizona. She'd also brought some clean underwear and a pair of turquoise scrubs decorated with teddy bears for Suze change into.

"More comfortable to sleep in than that gown."

"Thanks, Kath." Suze poked her head through the V-neck top. "For the scrubs and for being so supportive about Gabe and me getting back together. I know you were pretty pissed at me after the divorce."

Her sister-in-law acknowledged that with a unapologetic nod. "I thought you put your career ahead of your husband."

"You don't think I'm still doing that by letting Gabe give up his job and move back to Arizona with me?"

Kathy didn't reply for several moments. When she did, Suze caught a glimpse of pain in the hazel eyes so like her brother's.

"I've learned the hard way not to judge what goes on in anyone else's marriage. Don and I... Well, we've had some problems." She shook her head, as if to rid it of bad memories, and resumed her usual, brisk manner. "We're working through them, though, just like you and Gabe have had to work through yours. So you guys do whatever's right for the two of you, and to hell with what anyone else thinks."

Surprised and grateful, Suze returned her hug and thanked her again for the scrubs and the encouragement.

When Kathy left, Suze tried to rest. After the emotional upheaval of the day, she should've folded like a floppy-brimmed boonie hat. Instead she was restless and too wired to even doze.

The long nap with Gabe probably accounted for part of that restlessness. She picked up her cell phone but a glance at the clock showed it was almost ten, so she decided not to call. Hopefully, Gabe was already in bed and zoned out. She, on the other hand, had to get up and pee. Again.

Once up, she decided to wander down to the nurses' station in search of conversation and comfort food. The two females and one male on duty supplied her with both.

"I read about you in the paper," one of the nurses related. "I'd guess not many women get a Bronze Star."

"More than you think these days. Women account for close to twenty percent of Air Force, not quite as much in other branches of the service. They're pulling combat tours right alongside their male counterparts."

"My brother's a Marine," she volunteered. "He's with the 2nd Marine Expeditionary Force in Kandahar."

"Tough area," Suze commented with deliberate understatement.

The Taliban had regained a big patch of Kandahar. The province included the majority of Afghanistan's opium-producing poppy fields, which the terrorists used to fund their operations. Although the US-led coalition of NATO forces in Kandahar served as "advisors," they were right there, side by side with their counterparts, when the crap hit the fan.

The second female was more interested in Cedar Creek's hot young mayor.

"Is he as sexy as he looks?"

Suze laughed. "Sexier."

"Wow!"

She chatted with the evening crew for another ten or fifteen minutes. One Diet Dr Pepper and two ice cream cups later, she was still restless.

"What floor is the maternity ward on?"

"This floor, east wing. The nursery's viewing window will probably be curtained for the night, though."

Suze decided to take her chances. After her morning scare, she felt an undefined but deeply visceral need to connect with other mothers, other babies. Dropping her sister-in-law's name at the east wing's central station helped. The viewing window was, indeed curtained, but the flick of a switch opened it for a few precious moments.

The interior of the nursery remained dim, sheathing the plastic bassinets in soft light. Suze rested a palm on her stomach and let her gaze roam the high-tech cradles. Only three were occupied. The scrunch-faced occupants were all asleep. She watched them until Kathy's friend signaled that she needed to close the curtain and get back to her station.

Suze waved her thanks and meandered back to her own room. Still restless, she clicked on the TV and was watching an old movie with the soundtrack on low when she got a late visitor. The stranger didn't knock on the half-closed door, just poked her head inside.

"I heard your TV, Ms. Hall. May I come in?"

"Sure."

Suze understood why the woman hadn't knocked when she nudged the door open with one shoulder. Both arms were bandaged up to the elbow.

"I'm Donna Osborne," she said, confirming Suze's instant guess. "Your husband came to visit me earlier. He said you were here."

Suze clicked off the TV and swung her feet off the bed so she could sit up and face her visitor. "I'm so sorry about your husband."

Tears filmed the woman's tired eyes. "I still can't believe he's gone."

Suze was searching for the right words in the face of such raw grief when Donna Osborne showed she had a core of steel.

"I could've lost my boys, too," she said, blinking back her tears. "I almost did. So although all I want to do is howl and scream and pound my head against the wall, I have to be strong for them."

"How are they doing?"

"The oldest's burns are superficial, thank God. My mom flew in from Chicago this morning and will stay here at the healthplex with him. I'm transferring to Baptist tomorrow to be closer to my baby."

"I'm so sorry," Suze said again.

"Me, too." Donna let down her guard for a moment, and her face took on a haunted look. "It was such a stupid, stupid accident."

Suze could've said that, in her experience, most accidents were pretty damned stupid. Instead, she gestured to the chair beside her bed.

"Would you like to sit down?"

Donna pulled herself together again and shook her head. "No, I need to get back upstairs. I just wanted to thank you. Your husband told me what you did. To help put out the fire. I couldn't sleep wondering if you're in the hospital because of…because of us."

"No. It's something else entirely."

Donna nodded, obviously relived. "Well, that's one less guilt I have to carry on my heart. Whatever the problem is, I hope you're better soon."

"Thank you."

"And please tell your husband that I appreciate everything he's done for me and the boys more than I can ever say. I can't believe he's accomplished so much so quickly."

"He has?"

"He didn't tell you? He notified the insurance company for me. And talked to our church about organizing a clothing and toy drive. He's also assured me…" her eyes blurred again "…that someone from the medical examiner's office will contact me about when we can make funeral arrangements." She managed a wobbly smile. "He's a good man, Captain."

"I think so, too."

"Cedar Creek's lucky to have him."

Gabe was right, Suze thought when her unexpected visitor left. They *did* need to work on their communication skills. He hadn't told her about any of his activity on behalf of the Osbornes. Then again, she hadn't asked. Probably because she'd been so wrapped up in her own worries that she hadn't given any thought to his.

She lay awake as the clock ticked toward midnight, then one. Her body still sagged with residual tiredness but her mind swirled with everything that had happened in the past few days. The past few weeks, actually. In that short space of time, her world had turned upside down. So had Gabe's. And until this moment, they'd both been operating from their individual but separate perspectives.

Those searing few moments with Donna Osborne now had Suze reviewing every decision and questioning every step in the process. She finally dozed off and slept as well as anyone could in a hospital until her mom rapped lightly on her door.

"Hi, sweetie."

A quick glance at the clock showed it was barely six thirty. "Hi, Mom. What are you doing here so early?"

"Delivering the fresh-baked cinnamon-raisin rolls I promised. I wanted to be sure the night crew got some before they went off duty at seven. Dad's distributing them now. He'll be here in a minute."

"Hope he saves some for me!"

"Of course." She tipped her daughter a worried glance. "How did last night go? Any more spotting?"

"No."

"Thank God! Dad and I said some heavy prayers for you and our grandbaby."

"I said a few myself."

"Does Gabe know?"

"Not yet. I didn't want to call and wake him this early."

"Uh-oh. I called to tell him about the cinnamon rolls. He's on his way in. And I thought you might want to freshen up before he gets here." She dug into a tote splashed with embroidered hollyhocks almost as colorful as the streaks in her hair. "I brought you a hairbrush and a toothbrush. Some clean underwear, too, although it looks like you've already had a change of clothes."

"These are Kathy's scrubs. She brought them by before she went off duty last night."

"She's got a kind heart, even if she did say some rather disparaging things about you after the divorce."

"We talked about that."

Suze wanted to ask her mom if she'd heard anything about Kathy and her husband but refrained. That flash of pain she'd spotted in her sister-in-law's eyes made the topic too private, too personal.

Once she'd washed her face and brushed both her teeth and her hair, though, she did ask about Cedar Creek's community activities in support of Donna Osborne and her boys.

"The whole town's rallied," Mary Jackson reported. "For the Osbornes and the other families whose homes were damaged. The Kellys and the Sugarmans have moved into the Comfort Inn temporarily. We're having a bake sale at our church today to cover the cost of their rooms. The Methodist Church is soliciting contributions for Walmart gift cards so they can buy what they need in the interim, and Ruby's offered free meals until they get settled. Oh, and Alicia Johnson's been a whirlwind. As soon as she and Dave Forrester got back from Texas, she lined up rentals for both families and arm twisted the owners into giving the first three months rent free. I have to tell you, Suzanne, I could never warm up to Alicia when you were girls. And," she added with a sniff, "I certainly didn't like the way she threw herself at Gabe after the divorce. My opinion's changing, though."

"Mine, too."

"Really? What…? Oh, good. Here's your dad."

She jumped up to relieve him of an extra-large Tupperware carrier so he could give his daughter a kiss. "Cute teddy bears," he said, eyeing her borrowed scrubs. "Where'd you get them?"

"Kathy. She stopped by when she got off work last night." Suze twitched her nose, closed her eyes and floated on a heavenly scent. "Oh, my Lord, Mom. Those rolls smell incredible. Do we have to wait for Gabe?"

"Hell, yes, you do," her husband answered from the door.

He elbowed the door open, double-stacked coffee containers in both hands. He yielded the top ones from each hand to her parents before dropping a kiss on Suze's nose.

"Morning, wife."

"Morning, husband."

His gaze raked her face. "You look a little better than when I left you last night."

Suze wished she could say the same. He'd obviously showered and shaved, but the lines at the corners of his eyes and mouth seemed to have taken up permanent residence.

"Did you get any sleep last night?" she asked.

"Some. How about you?"

"Off and on."

"How's our little Peanut?"

The worry in his eyes belied the flippant question. A smile spread across her heart as she reassured him. "Still holding his or her own."

"So we're celebrating," her mom announced as she popped the top on the Tupperware container. "Sugar all around."

"Oh, Mary. Bless you."

Relief etched in every line of his face, Gabe closed his eyes and dragged in the scent of cinnamon, raisins and hundred-proof sugar icing.

"If I wasn't married to your daughter and your husband wasn't standing three feet away, I'd beg you to run away with me. All you'd have to do for the rest of your life is flip blueberry pecan pancakes and bake cinnamon rolls."

"Don't be so ridiculous." The scold didn't match her mom's delighted smile. "You don't need to suck up to me. You've already got my vote."

Suze knew her mother had tossed out the comment carelessly, without thinking. Yet the barb dug deep. She popped a soft, doughy bite studded with raisins and dripping with sugary frosting into her mouth, then reached for her coffee to wash it down. The brew was strong and black, just the way she liked it. Just the way Gabe always fixed it for her.

Without warning, her mind flashed back to their chance meeting in Arizona. The unplanned stop at McDonald's.

Her husband waiting with a coffee in each hand when she'd come out of the ladies' room. He'd remembered how she liked her coffee then, too. He'd remembered everything.

The confused, conflicting thoughts that had tumbled though her head during the sleepless hours last night coalesced. The brief, middle of the night talk with Donna Osborne had added a sharper focus to choices facing her and Gabe.

Like the bits of a thousand-piece jigsaw puzzle, they fell into place. And for the first time since she'd come home, Suze caught a clear, unclouded glimpse of her future.

She eased into it slowly, carefully. Between sips of the life-giving caffeine. "Donna Osborne came to see me last night."

"Seriously?" Gabe frowned. "She didn't look strong enough to get out of bed when I saw her yesterday afternoon."

"She was still in pretty bad shape. Both hands and arms were bandaged, and her grief seemed as though it was tearing her apart."

Her mom *tch-tched* in sympathy. "She and the boys will have a long road to recovery, emotionally and physically. Yesterday at the church we were talking about how we could help."

"Mom mentioned that Alicia has lined up rentals for the two families whose homes were damaged," Suze told Gabe. "Do you know if she's found anything for the Osbornes?"

"As a matter of fact, I was going to talk to you about that today." He polished off his roll and swiped his hands on a napkin. "I'd like to offer Donna my place until the boys are both well and she decides whether she's going to stay in Oklahoma or move back to Chicago to be closer to her folks. We'll be on our way to Arizona this time next week, so the timing should work."

"I thought of that, too, and it seemed like a perfect solution. There's just one problem."

"What's that?"

"You won't be going to Arizona."

The hand holding Gabe's coffee cup stopped halfway to his mouth. "You want to run that by me again?"

"I'm putting in my papers as soon as I get back to base."

Gabe went completely still, his eyes locked with hers. "When did you decide that?"

"Last night. After I talked to Donna Osborne."

"You don't think that's something we should discuss and decide together?"

The terse question turned her mom's expression from puzzled to worried. She glanced at her daughter, then her son-in-law and back again.

"What papers?" she wanted to know. "What are you talking about?"

They ignored her.

"I said last night we needed to improve our communications skills," Gabe said, each word clipped. "Maybe we should start with yours."

Flustered by the sudden tension in the air, her mom fisted her hands on her hips. "What papers, Suzanne?"

"C'mon, Mary." Her husband hooked a hand in her elbow and tugged her toward the door. "I'll explain outside. Let's get some fresh coffee and give them some privacy."

She went, but they could hear her wail from halfway down the corridor. "*What* papers?"

"Okay," Gabe said, his eyes still cool and flat. "It's just us, Suze. How about telling me why you've decided to separate from active duty and, oh, by the way, unilaterally reverse the course of our lives."

"Would you buy super-ultra-hyper hormones?"

"Suzanne…"

"Hey, it was worth a shot."

"Dammit!" His growl was all the more effective for being low and furious. "First you don't bother to tell me about the spotting. Now this?"

"I'm sorry, Gabe. I am, really. It was just so late, and Kathy said not to worry. And you were gone when I got up the next morning."

"Don't give me that bull. We both have cell phones, don't we?"

"Okay, I screwed up on that one." Sighing, she tipped her chin toward the chair pulled up next to the bed. "Can we at least sit down while I try to unscrew this one?"

She perched on the edge of the bed. Gabe faced her, his knees spaced between hers. His expression wasn't quite as taut as it had been a few moments ago but hadn't completely thawed yet.

"When I drove home to Oklahoma to tell you about the baby," she said slowly, trying to reduce her thoughts to an understandable logic, "I figured we'd work out amicable custody and visitation terms. And I knew you well enough to feel sure you'd take over as custodial parent if and when I deployed."

His lip curled. "Good to know you had such confidence in me."

"Okay, I deserve that. But I swear, Gabe, I never imagined, never *dreamed*, that you'd want to be such a big part of our baby's life that you'd quit your teaching job, resign as mayor and move to Arizona. Looking back, I think I was so surprised that I just grabbed at the offer with both hands."

"So what's changed?"

"Lots of things, but mostly my perception of the kind of the life we could build together in Cedar Creek."

She slicked her palms over her knees, then bridged the short distance from her thighs to his. His muscles were hard to her touch, his jeans stretched taut across them.

"You're a natural at your elected position, Mr. Mayor. You care, you're not afraid to get down and dirty, and you make things happen. Everyone says the next step is the state legislature. Then maybe the governor's office. But what's even more important to me is how you shape young minds."

She smiled at the memories.

"I kept thinking of the teachers who pushed and prodded me. Very Scary Mrs. Lee. Remember her?"

"Our seventh grade math teacher? Like I could forget."

"And my advanced physics prof our sophomore year at OU. If not for him, I wouldn't be an engineer—or be wearing captain's bars."

"Yeah, well, let's talk about those captain's bars. You said you intended to put in your papers. Does that mean you're quitting the Air Force completely? Or are you thinking about the Guard or Reserve?"

"I'd like to apply for the full-time vacancy coming up at the 137th. There's no guarantee I'll get it. I'm pretty junior compared to some of the folks out there. And if I do, I'll probably have to deploy at times, depending on the world crisis or natural disaster."

Gabe searched her face. He knew how much this intrepid woman thrived on challenges, the tougher the better. "What if you don't get the job at the 137th? What if you're stuck playing mommy in Cedar Creek for the rest of your life?"

As soon as the words were out, he realized how stupid they were.

"Oh, hell! Of course you won't stay stuck in Cedar Creek. If the 137th job doesn't pan out, you'll go to work for Dave Forrester and end up managing his entire conglomerate. Or get appointed to an international commission chartered to extract water from hot air in Africa. Or, hey, join the NASA team that wants to construct a laser highway to the moon."

Laughing, she didn't deny any of possibilities. "I'm thinking I could also lobby for the director of the EPA position when my husband wins a seat in the US Senate."

Gabe leaned forward and framed her face with his palms. "Tell me the truth, Suze. If the 137th job doesn't come through, can you really hang up your uniform with no regrets?"

"No regrets at all? Probably not. I love the camaraderie. And the sense of being part of something bigger than myself. You and the baby will just have to push me down a career path that provides that same level of satisfaction."

He blew a soundless whistle. "Looks like the kid and I have a job cut out for us."

"Yeah, you do." She angled her head and pressed a kiss on his palm. "So…are we good?"

"About staying in Cedar Creek? You know the answer to that. About how we got to that point? Not hardly."

His hand slid from her cheek to her chin. Curling his knuckles under her chin, he brushed his thumb across her lower lip. The touch was soft, sensual, but the look in his eyes was dead serious.

"It's not going to work if either one of us makes unilateral decisions on major issues like this one. We have to keep the comm lines open and humming."

She started to respond but his thumb pressed against her lips, halting her reply.

"We talk, Susie Q. About the baby. Our jobs. The price of a half gallon of Ben & Jerry's Cherry Garcia. Deal?"

"Deal."

## Chapter Twelve

Air Force regulations allowed Suze to request separation from active duty no earlier than ninety days and no later than thirty days prior to her expected delivery day. That meant she'd have six months yet at Luke AFB to train her replacement, apply for transition to the Reserves and get ready for another move. None of which, she insisted, was any big deal.

Nevertheless, Gabe requested a six-month leave of absence from his teaching and mayoral duties to accompany her. The school board was thrilled that he intended to return for the spring semester instead of quitting outright and happily approved the temporary absence. The members of Cedar Creek Town Council were just as accommodating. They approved Joanna Hicks as mayor *pro tem* but extracted a promise from Gabe to be immediately reachable by phone or computer if necessary.

When Suze tried one last time to suggest he wait for her here in Cedar Creek, Gabe shut her down. "We're not going through any more separations than we have to. Especially when you also have that uterine fibroid to take care of."

"Kathy says it's a simple outpatient laparoscopic procedure."

"Simple or not, I intend to be there. Besides, Doofus and I could use a break, right pal?"

The wire-haired griffon woofed his agreement.

"Ooooh boy," Suze laughed. "It's gonna be fun driving halfway across the country with Doofus occupying the back seat of my convertible, going crazy every time we pass a car or a truck."

"Ole Blue's got a trailer hitch. We'll tow the convertible and let Doofus reign supreme in the truck's jump seat."

"Like I said," Suze drawled, "it's gonna be fun."

Surprisingly, it was.

Before departing on their odyssey, they helped Donna Osborne, her mom and her oldest boy settle into the house. Donna still hadn't decided whether to remain in Cedar Creek or move closer to her parents. She had to put off thinking about that until her youngest had recovered and she'd sorted through the bewildering business of insurance claims for her home and her husband's death. The offer to live rent-free in Gabe's house for the next six months relieved her of one crushing problem.

They showed Donna through the house and gave her the keys late on a Thursday afternoon. The next morning they loaded up Ole Blue. Gabe had stashed most of his personal effects at Penny's house, so all he had to toss in the truck's lockable storage container was one duffle containing his clothes, the weekender roller bag Suzanne had brought for what she'd thought would be a short visit and a thirty-pound sack of dry dog food.

He stuffed his laptop and a thick wad of folders in a soft-sided briefcase. The case joined Suze's tote in the truck's air-conditioned cab. So did Doofus. Deliriously happy at the prospect of an outing, he left nose smears all over the narrow windows on both sides of the jump seat. As Suze had predicted, he took vocal exception to every moving object as they cruised down Main Street and headed for the interstate. Gabe finally shot him an evil look in the rearview mirror and warned of dire consequences—up to and including a visit to the vet for a too-long delayed snip—if he didn't lie down and shut up.

They hit I-40 and headed west. With each mile of undulating prairie, another boulder seemed to roll off their shoulders. Gabe, because this was his first hiatus from work since his election. Suze, because each passing moment confirmed the rightness of her decision.

They stopped to let Doofus do his thing in the dog-walking area at the rest stop just over the line into Texas. They stopped again for lunch in Amarillo. Since they couldn't leave the dog in a hot car, they drove through a Taco Bell and took their lunch to another highway rest stop. Two tacos each for Suze and Gabe, one as a treat for Doofus mixed in with his healthy-bones Purina chow. While they were stopped, Suze asked Gabe if he'd mind making a brief detour in Albuquerque.

"To visit Ben Kincaid and his wife?"

Suze nodded. "Ben wasn't there when I went through on the way out. I know he'd like to see us both."

Gabe readily agreed. Divorce, he'd discovered, tended to strain loyalties. He'd found it even more difficult to keep up with friends and acquaintances after he'd separated from the Air Force. Major Ben Kincaid was one of the few who'd made an effort to at least stay in touch.

"Yeah, sure, we can stop if they're going to be home." His grin slipped out. "I have to admit, I'd like to meet the woman who brought Love-'em-and-leave-'em-happy Ben Kincaid to his knees."

Alex Kincaid not only confirmed that they'd be home, the busy entrepreneur was thrilled to hear Suze was a bride. Again.

"Omigosh! You and your ex? Back together again? Wait until I tell Ben! He was bummed that he missed you on your way out to Oklahoma, and he said then that he wouldn't be surprised if the two of you hooked up again. He'll be *so* smug when he hears he was right."

"Are you sure it's convenient for us to stop by? I would've called earlier but…well…it's been kind of hectic. We just made the decision to pack up and head west two days ago."

"Heck, yes, it's convenient. You have to stay with us tonight. I want to hear every detail, Swish."

After almost ten days in her hometown, surrounded by family and friends who knew her only as Suzanne or Suze, hearing her military call sign again gave her a little jolt.

"We can't stay the night, Alex. We have a very large, very noisy hound accompanying us, so we booked a room at a pet-friendly hotel west of Albuquerque."

"At least stay for dinner," Alex pleaded. "Ben can

throw some steaks on the grill and share his latest war stories with you while *I* get acquainted with the guy who's so hot you married him twice."

Suze had to laugh. "And he's looking forward to meeting the gal who shot Cowboy down in flames."

"Great! Call us when you hit the outskirts of town and we'll fire up the grill. Oh, and bring the dog in with you. Our backyard isn't all that big but it's enclosed. Maria will love playing with him."

"But her cat probably not so much."

"So Sox can stay inside. See you soon."

The evening was one of the most relaxing Suze had spent in months. Make that years. She and her husband, together again, seated at a table with a view through French doors of a backyard landscaped in gorgeous high-desert style, sharing laughter and lusciously marinated steaks and the company of another couple obviously devoted to each other. Cowboy had stopped on his way home to buy a couple of bottles of nonalcoholic sparkling cider to celebrate both the remarriage and the baby. The four of them lingered at the table, enjoying the bubbly, long after the dishes were cleared.

Outside, Maria shrieked in delight as Doofus frolicked with her in the sprinkler Ben had set up for them. Delirious with joy, the dog barked his fool head off and did a leaping, contorted jig as he tried to plant his huge paws over the water spouts. Maria's cat was not amused. She sat on a windowsill in the kitchen, her tail twitching back and forth and her eyes narrowed to slits as she monitored the outdoor activities.

The adults had kept the conversation general while Maria was with them. Once the girl went outside, Cowboy turned the talk back to Suze's surprise announcement that she intended to separate from active duty, move back to her hometown and go into the Reserves. Not unexpectedly, his reaction was mixed. He was still Special Ops. Still gung-ho. But marriage and a ready-made family had given him a decidedly different perspective on the demands of a military career. After some back and forth, he reluctantly admitted that being a full-time Air Reserve Technician and member of an Air Guard unit with a distinguished combat record like that of the 137th would make use of Swish's training, experience and leadership skills.

Alex endorsed his opinion. "Looks like a win-win situation to me," she said as she grimaced and shifted on her cushioned chair. When she caught Swish's glance, she laughed. "I thought the second trimester was a pain in the you know what. It's got nothing on the third."

"Bad, huh?"

"Just your average backaches from hell, spider veins, swollen ankles and heartburn. Which is exactly what I tried to tell Chelsea."

"Has she been up to visit lately?"

"No, but I talk to her at least once a week."

"Who's Chelsea?" Gabe wanted to know.

"Oh, sorry. She was my roommate when I lived in Vegas," Alex explained. "I forgot you weren't at the last Badger Bash. You would've met her there. She's a dancer. A good one, although she's currently between gigs."

"She won't be unemployed long." Her husband grinned. "The woman is five nine, most of it leg, and built like the proverbial brick..."

"Care...*ful*!"

"Let's just says she's built."

"She's the one who's got a sort of on-again, off-again going with Dingo," Suze put in.

"Okay, got it," Gabe said. "I remember you mentioning something about that. So is it on now or off?"

"We're not sure. Chelsea hasn't said, and no one's heard from Dingo."

Suze and the lively dancer hadn't spent all that much time together at the Bash but she'd admired her liveliness and outspoken personality. Chelsea Howard was out there, literally and figuratively.

"So, what's she up to if she's not working?" she asked between sips of sweetened iced tea.

Alex threw a quick glance at her still-splashing daughter, then heaved a sigh. "She's decided to have a baby."

Suze snorted into her tea. "Good grief! This baby thing is spreading like a virus!"

"She read some article about inherited genetic traits in *Scientific American*," Cowboy said with another grin.

"*Scientific American?* Really?"

"Hey, she's not all hair and long legs," Alex put in loyally.

Cowboy picked up the narrative again. "She figures with her talent and undeniably spectacular looks, she could mate her DNA with that of a certified genius and hit the baby jackpot."

"Is that all she wants to mate? Their DNA?"

"Apparently." Cowboy's blue eyes glinted with laughter. "She's drawn up a list of candidates and plans to start interviewing them between auditions for another gig."

"Are you serious?"

"As a mortar attack."

"I need to meet this woman," Gabe commented to no one in particular.

"She's going to fly up for a visit when she narrows the list to the final three. To get Alex's input."

"Is she talking artificial insemination?"

"I'm not sure. I'm almost afraid to... Oh!"

She sat up, her eyes wide, and flattened both palms on her belly. Stiffening, Cowboy went on full alert until Alex slumped against her chair again.

"Whew! That was a good one. Braxton Hicks contractions," she explained to her startled guests. "I've had them intermittently for a while but they're getting more frequent. My doc says that's common in pre-labor. The cervix is preparing for delivery."

Her husband was already on his feet and cupping his wife's arm. "Let's you into a more comfortable chair. Swish, how about you keep Alex company in the other room while Gabe and I pull kitchen duty, then get Maria and the hound dried off?"

She was only too happy to agree. After her own scares with spotting, she intended to pump Alex for any and all information she wanted to share about this life-altering condition.

She and Gabe and Doofus said goodbye just a little more than an hour later. They weren't about to overstay their welcome in the face of their hostess's obvious discomfort and the hissing hostility of Maria's cat to the canine invasion of her territory.

Before they left, Alex presented Swish with another of her personally designed tees. This one was done in camouflage colors and featured a glittering American eagle with wings folded to shelter its chick. Its talons clutched a banner with a fierce warning: Don't Mess with an Air Force Mom.

"I've designed one for each branch of the service," Alex related. "I put the designs up on my website two days ago and we're already swamped with orders."

"I love it! But you have to let me pay for it."

"Just wear it around your base. We'll consider the free advertising as payment in kind."

"You got it."

Doofus, who'd bonded with Maria, vociferously protested being herded into Ole Blue. Over his mournful howls at being separated from his new best pal, Swish gave Alex a final hug and a strict order.

"Call us if those fake contractions turn real and you guys need babysitting or hand-holding service. Gabe or I or both can jump a plane and be here in a few hours."

"Thanks. I'll remember that. And same goes for you, Warrior Mom. One call, and either Ben or I will be there."

It took close to forty minutes to navigate Albuquerque's traffic, pick up I-40 again and reach the hotel situated just across the Rio Grande. By then, Doofus couldn't wait to get out and explore the empty acres behind the hotel. Gabe kept him on a long, retractable leash, which he strenuously objected to. So much so that they were both hot and bothered when they returned to the hotel room.

"I've already hit the shower," Swish said while the hound slurped water from his dish.

She stretched out on the bed and was half dozing when Gabe emerged. He'd wrapped a towel around his hips, giving her a bird's-eye view of several interesting inches of pale belly below his tan line. His dark-brown hair still glistened with damp, and the glint in his hazel eyes started her heart humming in her throat.

Oh, God, he was gorgeous. Not the *GQ* kind of gorgeous, all suave and slick and styled. Or the muscled-up Navy SEAL kind. Just your average lean, tanned, smart, funny, thoughtful, kind type of gorgeous.

She wanted him so bad she hurt with it. But they'd decided to take it slow and careful until she consulted her doc. That decision was now slapping smack up against the desire coiling in her belly.

"Here's the deal," she told him, her voice husky. "You can drop that towel and make cautious, careful love to your wife. Or..."

"Or?"

"Or you can drop the towel and let me make wild, crazy love to my husband."

"There's a third option." He waggled his brows in an exaggerated leer. "How about you lie back, close your eyes and let me demonstrate the various ways a husband can pleasure his wife using only his hands, his tongue and his imagination?"

She wasn't going to argue with that!

Her pulse kicking into overdrive, she threw aside the light comforter she'd drawn over herself after the shower. The abrupt movement sent an unmistakable signal to Doofus. He'd been snoozing in a corner but now, sensing action, he charged across the room. Snagging a corner of the comforter, he dragged it completely off. His tail slashed back and forth. His teeth showed in a goofy grin as he waited for his humans to initiate his favorite game. When they ignored him, he whined once. Twice. Raked the mattress with an insistent paw.

He rocked back on his haunches, preparing to join

the fun on the bed, but Gabe sensed what was coming and paused in his imaginative efforts long enough to bellow a warning.

"No! Do not even *think* about it!"

Deterred but not completely cowed, the hound circled a few times, pawed the comforter into an acceptable nest, settled in and glared at his humans from the floor.

Suze was totally oblivious to their audience of one. True to his word, Gabe had exercised his very inventive imagination. She was writhing. Panting. Gripping the pillow with both hands. As the exquisite sensations rose and fell and rose again, she tried to hold back. Tried to spin them out. But the high, wild waves crested. One after another. Then came crashing down.

When her mind reinhabited her body, Gabe had eased up beside her. His right arm snaked under her shoulders. His left palm flattened on her belly.

"Wonder what Peanut thinks just happened?" he mused.

*"Please,"* she groaned. "Don't go there. I won't be ready to explain what just happened until the kid is in his or her teens."

"Better not wait that long. My crush on you went from bashful to excruciating the first week I hit puberty. I spent that entire damned school year trying to disguise my hard-on every time you sashayed by."

"Ha! You wouldn't know bashful if it hit you in the face. But since we're being honest here, I'll come clean, too." She curved a palm against his cheek and answered his questioning look with a sly smile. "Why do you think my hip swing kicked into fourth gear every time I caught you watching me?"

"C'mon. You couldn't have known the agonies I was going through. Not at that age."

"Shows what you know. That bulge in your jeans fueled more erotic fantasies than any of the steamy novels I snuck out of the library."

"Christ, Suze." He curled his arm, drawing her closer. "With two oversexed parents like us, Peanut doesn't have a chance."

Laughing, she laid her hand atop the one resting on her belly. After all the months and years apart, after all the loneliness and regrets and stress, she and Gabe were right where they were supposed to be. Wrapped in each other's arms. His breath warm on her heated skin. Her hand coupled with his.

Whatever happened, whatever bumps and detours they had to face in the years ahead, this was exactly where they would stay.

## Chapter Thirteen

Almost a year later, Suze grinned as she skimmed the text message that popped up on her iPhone screen.

From: Gator
To: Swish
Hey, girl! Cowboy, Kojack, Barbie, Dingo & Elvis already here. Where U at?

"Gator wants to know where we are," she relayed to her husband.

Gabe glanced her way, sunlight glinting off his aviator sunglasses. His left elbow rested on the open driver's-side window while he steered their rented Jeep Wrangler along California's fabled Highway 1. Big Sur splashed and crashed far below on their left. The rumpled, drought-parched Santa Lucia Mountains crowded close on their right. Thankfully, the massive landslide that had shut down a twelve-mile section of the highway south of Monterey last year had been cleared. They'd made good time since picking up the Jeep at LAX and heading north.

"Tell him we're about ten miles out."

Her thumbs worked. X-Man says 10 miles out.

The answer came back a few seconds later. Beer's on ice. Haul ass.

Still grinning, she clicked off the phone and dropped it in the armrest's cupholder. She could hardly believe another Badger Bash had rolled around. Or that she'd left the last one, spent what was left of the night shooting the breeze with her Air Force pals, then driven home through the just-breaking Arizona dawn, only to pull up at a red light and spot her ex-husband's truck across the intersection.

Her ex-ex now. The designation had tickled her. So much she'd started calling him XX, which quickly morphed to X-Man. Their family and friends had quickly picked up the tag. His students loved it, too, although none would dare use it to his face. Even the members of the town council had taken to calling him Mayor X-Man.

She stretched in her seat, enjoying the breeze from the open window and trying not to worry too much about Ellie, aka the Peanut. This was the first time they'd left their three-month-old for longer than one night. Granted, her parents had plenty of backup with Gabe's sisters and their husbands close by. And, as Suze's mother reminded her when she'd shooed her daughter out the door, Doofus would remain on duty. The hound was totally, completely goofy about the baby. And so fiercely protective no stranger got within twenty yards of Peanut until they'd been thoroughly vetted.

Suze had quashed her maternal doubts and told herself that this short weekend jaunt would be a good first step in dealing with any incipient separation anxiety. It would also help condition her for an upcoming two-week deployment to a classified location that she and a small cadre from the 137th had been tapped for.

Her transition to full-time Air Reservist had come faster and gone smoother than she'd anticipated. The slot Colonel Amistad had discussed with her had opened up less than two months after Ellie's birth. The competition for it had been fierce, but Swish's training and experience during her years on active duty gave her an edge. She was back in uniform again, doing what she loved and going home most evenings to her husband and daughter.

Life was good. Very good.

The breeze tugged at the hair she'd pulled through the opening in the back of her cap. It was another Alexis Scott creation, bling-studded and sparkling in the bright sunlight. She and Alex had become close this past year, communicating regularly via text, email and Facebook on the joys and challenges of motherhood.

"It'll be great to see Alex and Cowboy again," she commented to Gabe. "I was surprised when she told me they weren't bringing either Maria or little Ben with them, though."

"Guess they needed some adult time." Gabe glanced her way again and waggled his brows above the rim of his sunglasses. "I have to admit, I'm looking forward to it, too. Particularly the part that comes after this beach bash Gator's organized."

"The hotel's right on the beach. Nothing says we can't slip away whenever the mood strikes us. Or…" She matched his leer. "I seem to recall getting lost in the sand dunes with you once or twice when we were stationed in North Carolina."

"Either option works for me."

The Bash was in full swing by the time they checked into their hotel room, dumped their bags and changed into cutoffs and tank tops. Following the sound of laughter, they took the wooden stairs leading to the half-moon cove that thousands of years of pounding waves had carved out of the cliffs.

A dozen or so people now laid claim to the narrow stretch of pebbly beach fringing the cove. Wooden Adirondack chairs weathered to a silvery gray had been arranged in a circle around a stone fire pit, already lit and dancing with flames. Buckets and trays of appetizers provided by the hotel were being passed around. As Suze and Gabe descended the stairs, they caught snatches of raucous laughter as the chairs' occupants vied with each other to recount ever more improbable exploits of Colonel Bob Dolan, aka Badger.

The organizer of this year's Bash caught sight of them first. Interrupting the tales, he called a greeting. "Yo! Swish. X-Man. 'Bout time you two got here."

Gator lifted his wife off his knee and heaved out of the low-slung chair. After enveloping Swish in a bear hug, he pounded Gabe on the back and gestured to the others with his dew-streaked beer bottle.

"Y'all know everybody."

Almost everybody, she corrected with a quick sweep of the small crowd. There were a few unfamiliar faces. Kojack's new wife was one. Barbie Doll's fiancé was another. After quick introductions, Gabe went to retrieve two beers while Swish perched on the arm of Dingo's chair. He was sprawled next to Alex and Cowboy, his legs thrust toward the fire pit. Despite his lazy slouch, though, Swish picked up a tense vibe.

"You okay?" she asked, nudging his knee with hers. "You look a little tight around the edges."

"I'm good."

The terse reply arced her brows. She looked a question at Alex, who answered it with one word. "Chelsea."

"Uh-oh."

From her conversations with Alex over the past twelve months, Suze knew the vivacious showgirl's on-again, off-again relationship with Dingo was currently off. She also knew Chelsea had become a fierce advocate for a new cause. She no longer aspired to join the ranks of single mothers. In one of those too-weird-to-be-believed encounters that had even the Vegas police shaking their heads, she'd accidentally rescued a fifteen-year old sex slave. Horrified by the girl's situation, Chelsea had now turned her formidable energy to busting up human trafficking rings.

Drawing Swish a little way apart, Alex relayed the latest news in a soft murmur. "Chelsea's decided to go undercover. And she wants Dingo to pose as her pimp or procurer or whatever the heck they call it in the trafficking business."

"Oh, God! Please tell me you're kidding."

"I wish I could."

"Dingo *can't* have agreed to go along with that crazy scheme."

"Chelsea says he threatened to wring her neck first. But you know how…"

"Whoa!"

The startled exclamation cut through their quiet conversation and jerked them around. Like everyone else on the tiny slice of beach, they gaped at the woman descending the wooden stairs.

Her cutoffs were probably illegal in at least a half-dozen states. Their ragged fringe had to tickle her crotch. But they also showed off disgustingly trim thighs that other women would kill for. The V of her stretchy, sleeveless top revealed a deeper crevass than the Grand Canyon, and its rib-kissing hem displayed even more skin, including a diamond belly button stud that caught the setting sun and flashed fire with every step.

For several frozen moments, the awed silence was broken only by the sputter and hiss of the fire and the wash of waves against the pebbled shore. Then Dingo bolted out of his chair and made for the stairs.

Suze was still transfixed by the scene when Gabe appeared at her side to murmur, "That, I presume, is Chelsea."

"You presume correctly."

In a quiet undertone she related the dancer's hopes to draw Dingo into undercover work with her.

Gabe's lips pursed in a soundless whistle. "I sure as hell don't envy him the next few months."

He handed her an icy bottle and clinked his own against it. A shift of his shoulders blocked everything else from her view. The fire. The shadowed cliffs surrounding the cove. The small drama currently taking place at the bottom of the stairs.

"Did I ever thank you, Susie Q?"

His voice was a soft, erotic caress backed by the murmur of the sea. She shivered and smiled her delight. "For?"

"For being sane, sensible, uncrazy you. And for loving me."

"You have, actually. But if you want to express your

appreciation again, we could slip away for that quality adult time we talked about earlier."

Grinning, he plucked her beer out of her hand and plunked it down next to his on the arm of Dingo's vacated chair. Since everyone else's attention was still riveted on the showgirl and the ex-cop, he drew her away from the circle of chairs.

They picked their way along the rocky shore until the cliffs towered a hundred feet or more above them. The nooks and crannies carved by the relentless sea provided a good measure of privacy, but not enough for either one of them to risk a public indecency charge.

Gabe settled for propping his shoulders against a rocky wall and tugging off his wife's sparkly hat. Her ash-blond hair tumbled over her shoulders, and her green eyes were as deep and beguiling as the ocean.

She leaned back against the circle of his arms and smiled up at him. "I still can't believe everything that's happened since last year's Bash. You. Me. Ellie. Alex and Maria and the two Bens, big and small. If the next year is as hectic as this last one, I don't know if I can handle it."

"You can handle anything." He raked back the hair at her temples and framed her face with his palms. "Now, how about you forget Ellie and Alex and the two Bens and just kiss me, Captain."

\* \* \* \* \*

*Don't miss Alex and Ben's story:*
MARRY ME, MAJOR
*Available now!*

*And for more great military romances,*
*try these other* AMERICAN HEROES *books:*

THE LIEUTENANT'S ONLINE LOVE
*by Caro Carson*

SOLDIER, HANDYMAN, FAMILY MAN
*by Lynne Marshal*

A PROPOSAL FOR THE OFFICER
*by Christy Jeffries*

*Available wherever Harlequin Special Edition*
*books and ebooks are sold!*

Turn the page for a sneak peek at the latest entry in
New York Times *bestselling author*
*RaeAnne Thayne's*
HAVEN POINT *series*,
*THE COTTAGES ON SILVER BEACH,*
*the story of a disgraced FBI agent,*
*his best friend's sister and the loss that affected*
*the trajectory of both their lives,*
*available July 2018*
*wherever HQN books and ebooks are sold!*

# *CHAPTER ONE*

SOMEONE WAS TRYING to bust into the cottages next door.

Only minutes earlier, Megan Hamilton had been minding her own business, sitting on her front porch, gazing out at the stars and enjoying the peculiar quiet sweetness of a late-May evening on Lake Haven. She had earned this moment of peace after working all day at the inn's front desk then spending the last four hours at her computer, editing photographs from Joe and Lucy White's 50th anniversary party the weekend before.

Her neck was sore, her shoulders tight, and she simply wanted to savor the purity of the evening with her dog at her feet. Her moment of Zen had lasted only sixty seconds before her little ancient pug Cyrus sat up, gazed out into the darkness and gave one small harrumphing noise before settling back down again to watch as a vehicle pulled up to the cottage next door.

Cyrus had become used to the comings and goings of their guests in the two years since he and Megan moved into the cottage after the inn's renovations were finished. She would venture to say her pudgy little dog seemed to actually enjoy the parade of strangers who invariably stopped to greet him.

The man next door wasn't aware of her presence, though, or that of her little pug. He was too busy trying to work the finicky lock—not an easy feat as the task typically took two hands and one of his appeared to be attached to an arm tucked into a sling.

She should probably go help him. He was obviously struggling one-handed, unable to turn the key and twist the knob at the same time.

Beyond common courtesy, there was another compelling reason she should probably get off her porch swing and assist him. He was a guest of the inn, which meant he was yet one more responsibility on her shoulders. She knew the foibles of that door handle well, since she owned the door, the porch, the house and the land that it sat on, here at Silver Beach on Lake Haven, part of the extensive grounds of the Inn at Haven Point.

She didn't want to help him. She wanted to stay right here hidden in shadows, trying to pretend he wasn't there. Maybe this was all a bad dream and she wouldn't be stuck with him for the next three weeks.

Megan closed her eyes, wishing she could open them again and find the whole thing was a figment of her imagination.

Unfortunately, it was all entirely too real. Elliot Bailey. Living next door.

She didn't want him here. Stupid online bookings. If he had called in person about renting the cottage next to hers—one of five small, charming two-bedroom vacation rentals along the lakeshore—she might have been able to concoct some excuse.

With her imagination, surely she could have come up with something good. All the cottages were being painted. A plumbing issue meant none of them had water. The entire place had to be fumigated for tarantulas.

If she had spoken with him in person, she may have been able to concoct *some* excuse that would keep Elliot Bailey away. But he had used the inn's online reservation system and paid in full before she even realized who was moving in next door. Now she was stuck with him for three entire weeks.

She would have to make the best of it.

As he tried the door again, guilt poked at her. Even if she didn't want him here, she couldn't sit here when one of her guests needed help. It was rude, selfish and irresponsible. "Stay," she murmured to Cyrus, then stood up and made her way down the porch steps of Primrose Cottage and back up those of Cedarwood.

"May I help?"

At her words, Elliot whirled around, the fingers of his right hand flexing inside his sling as if reaching for a weapon. She had to hope he didn't have one. Maybe she should have thought of that before sneaking up on him.

Elliot was a decorated FBI agent and always exuded an air of cold danger, as if ready to strike at any moment. It was as much a part of him as his blue eyes.

His brother had shared the same eyes, but the similarities between them ended there. Wyatt's blue eyes had been warm, alive, brimming with personality. Elliot's were serious and solemn and always seemed to look at her as if she were some kind of alien life-form that had landed in his world.

Her heart gave a familiar pinch at the thought of Wyatt and the fledgling dreams that had been taken away from her on a snowy road.

"Megan," he said, his voice as stiff and formal as if he were greeting J. Edgar Hoover himself. "I didn't see you."

"It's a dark evening and I'm easy to miss. I didn't mean to startle you."

In the yellow glow of the porch light, his features appeared lean and alert, like a hungry mountain lion. She could feel her muscles tense in response, a helpless doe caught unawares in an alpine meadow.

She adored the rest of the Bailey family. All of them, even linebacker-big Marshall. Why was Elliot the only one who made her so blasted nervous?

"May I help you?" she asked again. "This lock can be sticky. Usually it takes two hands, one to twist the key and the other to pull the door toward you."

"That could be an issue for the next three weeks." His voice seemed flat and she had the vague, somewhat disconcerting impression that he was tired. Elliot always seemed so invincible but now lines bracketed his mouth and his hair was uncharacteristically rumpled. It seemed so odd to see him as anything other than perfectly controlled.

Of course he was tired. The man had just driven in from Denver. Anybody would be exhausted after an eight-hour drive—especially when he was healing from an obvious injury and probably in pain.

What happened to his arm? She wanted to ask, but couldn't quite find the courage. It wasn't her business anyway. Elliot was a guest of her inn and deserved all the hospitality she offered to any guest—including whatever privacy he needed and help accessing the cottage he had paid in advance to rent.

"There is a trick," she told him. "If you pull the door slightly toward you first, then turn the key, you should be able to manage with one hand. If you have trouble again, you can find me or one of the staff to help you. I live next door."

The sound he made might have been a laugh or a scoff. She couldn't tell.

"Of course you do."

She frowned. What did that mean? With all the renovations to the inn after a devastating fire, she couldn't afford to pay for an overnight manager. It had seemed easier to move into one of the cottages so she could be close enough to step in if the front desk clerks had a problem in the middle of the night.

That's the only reason she was here. Elliot didn't need to respond to that information as if she was some loser who hadn't been able to fly far from the nest.

"We need someone on-site full-time to handle emergencies," she said stiffly. "Such as guests who can't open their doors by themselves."

"I am certainly not about to bother you or your staff every time I need to go in and out of my own rental unit. I'll figure something out."

His voice sounded tight, annoyed, and she tried to attribute it to travel weariness instead of that subtle disapproval she always seemed to feel emanating from him.

"I can help you this time at least." She inserted his key, exerted only a slight amount of pull on the door and heard the lock disengage. She pushed the door open and flipped on a light inside the cheery little two-bedroom cottage, with its small combined living-dining room and kitchen table set in front of the big windows over-looking the lake.

"Thank you for your help," he said, sounding a little less censorious.

"Anytime." She smiled her well-practiced, smooth, innkeeper smile. After a decade of running the twenty-room Inn at Haven Point on her own, she had become quite adept at exuding hospitality she was far from feeling.

"May I help you with your bags?"

He gave her a long, steady look that conveyed clearly what he thought of that offer. "I'm good. Thanks."

She shrugged. Stubborn man. Let him struggle. "Good night, then. If you need anything, you know where to find me."

"Yes. I do. Next door, apparently."

"That's right. Good night," she said again, then returned to her front porch, where she and Cyrus settled in to watch him pull a few things out of his vehicle and carry them inside.

She could have saved him a few trips up and down those steps, but clearly he wanted to cling to his own stubbornness instead. As usual, it was obvious he wanted nothing to do with her. Elliot tended to treat her as if she were a riddle he had no desire to solve.

Over the years, she had developed pretty good strategies for avoiding him at social gatherings, though it was a struggle. She had once been almost engaged to his younger brother. That alone would tend to link her to the Bailey family, but it wasn't the only tie between them. She counted his sisters, Wynona Bailey Emmett and Katrina Bailey Callahan, among her closest friends.

In fact, because of her connection to his sisters, she knew he was in town at least partly to attend a big after-the-fact reception to celebrate Katrina's wedding to Bowie Callahan, which had been a small destination event in Colombia several months earlier.

Megan had known Elliot for years. Though only five or six years older, somehow he had always seemed ancient to her, even when she was a girl—as if he belonged to some earlier generation. He was so serious all the time, like some sort of stuffy uncle who couldn't be bothered with youthful shenanigans.

*Hey, you kids. Get off my lawn.*

He'd probably never actually said those words, but she could clearly imagine them coming out of that incongruously sexy mouth.

He did love his family. She couldn't argue that. He watched out for his sisters and was close to his brother Marshall, the sheriff of Lake Haven County. He cherished his mother and made the long trip from Denver to Haven Point for every important Bailey event, several times a year.

Which also begged the question, why had he chosen to rent a cottage on the inn property instead of staying with one of his family members?

His mother and stepfather lived not far away and so did Marshall, Wynona and Katrina with their respective spouses. While Marshall's house was filled to the brim with kids, Cade and Wyn had plenty of room and Bowie and Katrina had a vast house on Serenity Harbor that would fit the entire Haven Point High School football team, with room left over for the coaching staff and a few cheerleaders.

Instead, Elliot had chosen to book this small, solitary rental unit at the inn for three entire weeks.

Did his reasons have anything to do with that sling? How had he been hurt? Did it have anything to do with his work for the FBI?

None of her business, Megan reminded herself. He was a guest at her inn, which meant she had an obligation to respect his privacy.

He came back to the vehicle for one more bag, something that looked the size of a laptop, which gave her something else to consider. He had booked the cottage for three weeks. Maybe he had taken a leave of absence or something to work on another book.

She pulled Cyrus into her lap and rubbed behind his ears as she considered the cottage next door and the enigmatic man currently inhabiting it. Whoever would have guessed that the stiff, humorless, focused FBI agent could pen gripping true crime books in his spare time? She would never admit it to Elliot, but she found it utterly fascinating how his writing managed to convey pathos and drama and even some lighter moments.

True crime was definitely not her groove at all but she had read his last bestseller in five hours, without so much as stopping to take a bathroom break—and had slept with her closet light on for weeks.

That still didn't mean she wanted him living next door. At this point, she couldn't do anything to change that. The only thing she could do was treat him with the same courtesy and respect she would any other guest at the inn.

No matter how difficult that might prove.

WHAT THE HELL was he doing here?

Elliot dragged his duffel to the larger of the cottage's two bedrooms, where a folding wood-framed luggage stand had been set out, ready for guests.

The cottage was tastefully decorated in what he termed Western chic—bold mission furniture, wood plank ceiling, colorful rugs on the floor. A river rock fireplace dominated the living room, probably perfect for those chilly evenings along the lakeshore.

Cedarwood Cottage seemed comfortable and welcoming, a good place for him to huddle over his laptop and pound out the last few chapters of the book that was overdue to his editor.

Even so, he could already tell this was a mistake.

Why the hell hadn't he just told his mother and Katrina he couldn't make it to the reception? He'd flown to Cartagena for the wedding three months earlier, after all. Surely that showed enough personal commitment to his baby sister's nuptials.

They would have protested but would have understood—and in the end it wouldn't have much mattered whether he made it home for the event or not. The reception wasn't about him, it was about Bowie and Katrina and the life they were building with Bowie's younger brother Milo and Kat's adopted daughter, Gabriella.

For his part, Elliot was quite sure he would have been better off if he had stayed holed up in his condo in Denver to finish the book, no matter how awkward things had become for him there. If he closed the blinds, ignored the doorbell and just hunkered down, he could have typed one-handed or even dictated the changes he needed to make. The whole thing would have been done in a week.

The manuscript wasn't the problem.

Elliot frowned, his head pounding in rhythm to each throbbing ache of his shoulder.

*He* was the problem—and he couldn't escape the mess he had created, no matter how far away from Denver he drove.

He struggled to unzip the duffel one-handed, then finally gave up and stuck his right arm out of the sling to help. His shoulder ached even more in response, not happy with being subjected to eight hours of driving only days postsurgery.

How was he going to explain the shoulder injury to his mother? He couldn't tell her he was recovering from a gunshot wound. Charlene had lost a son and husband in the line of duty and had seen both a daughter and her other son injured on the job.

And he certainly couldn't tell Marshall or Cade about all the trouble he was in. He was the model FBI agent, with the unblemished record.

Until now.

Unpacking took him all of five minutes, moving the packing cubes into drawers, setting his toiletries in the bathroom, hanging the few dress shirts he had brought along. When he was done, he wandered back into the combined living room/kitchen.

The front wall was made almost entirely of windows, perfect for looking out and enjoying the spectacular view of Lake Haven during one of its most beautiful seasons, late spring, before the tourist horde descended.

On impulse, Elliot walked out onto the wide front porch. The night was chilly but the mingled scents of pine and cedar and lake intoxicated him. He drew fresh mountain air deep into his lungs.

This.

If he needed to look for a reason why he had been compelled to come home during his suspension and the investigation into his actions, he only had to think about what this view would look like in the morning, with the sun creeping over the mountains.

Lake Haven called to him like nowhere else on Earth—not just the stunning blue waters or the mountains that jutted out of them in jagged peaks but the calm, rhythmic lapping of the water against the shore, the ever-changing sky, the cry of wood ducks pedaling in for a landing.

He had spent his entire professional life digging into the worst aspects of the human condition, investigating cruelty and injustice and people with no moral conscience whatsoever. No matter what sort of muck he waded through, he had figured out early in his career at the FBI that he could keep that ugliness from touching the core of him with thoughts of Haven Point and the people he loved who called this place home.

He didn't visit as often as he would like. Between his job at the Denver field office and the six true crime books he had written, he didn't have much free time.

That all might be about to change. He might have more free time than he knew what to do with.

His shoulder throbbed again and he adjusted the sling, gazing out at the stars that had begun to sparkle above the lake.

After hitting rock bottom professionally, with his entire future at the FBI in doubt, where else would he come but home?

He sighed and turned to go back inside. As he did, he spotted the lights still gleaming at the cottage next door, with its blue trim and the porch swing overlooking the water.

She wasn't there now.

Megan Hamilton. Auburn hair, green eyes, a smile that always seemed soft and genuine to everyone else but him.

He drew in a breath, aware of a sharp little twinge of hunger deep in his gut.

When he booked the cottage, he hadn't really thought things through. He should have remembered that Megan and the Inn at Haven Point were a package deal. She owned the inn along with these picturesque little guest cottages on Silver Beach.

He had no idea she actually *lived* in one herself, though. If he had ever heard that little fact, he had forgotten it. Should he have remembered, he would have looked a little harder for a short-term rental property, rather than picking the most convenient lakeshore unit he had found.

Usually, Elliot did his best to avoid her. He wasn't sure why but Megan always left him…unsettled. It had been that way for ages, since long before he learned she and his younger brother had started dating.

He could still remember his shock when he came home for some event or other and saw her and Wyatt together. As in, together, together. Holding hands, sneaking the occasional kiss, giving each other secret smiles. Elliot had felt as if Wyatt had peppered him with buckshot.

He had tried to be happy for his younger brother, one of the most generous, helpful, loving people he'd ever known. Wyatt had been a genuinely good person and deserved to be happy with someone special.

Elliot had felt small and selfish for wishing that someone hadn't been Megan Hamilton.

Watching their glowing happiness together had been tough. He had stayed away for the four or five months they had been dating, though he tried to convince himself it hadn't been on purpose. Work had been demanding and he had been busy carving out his place in the Bureau. He had also started the research that would become his first book, looking into a long-forgotten Montana case from a century earlier where a man had wooed, then married, then killed three spinster schoolteachers from back East for their life insurance money before finally being apprehended by a savvy local sheriff and the sister of one of the dead women.

The few times Elliot returned home during the time Megan had been dating his brother, he had been forced to endure family gatherings knowing she would be there, upsetting his equilibrium and stealing any peace he usually found here.

He couldn't let her do it to him this time.

Her porch light switched off a moment later and Elliot finally breathed a sigh of relief.

He would only be here three weeks. Twenty-one days. Despite the proximity of his cabin to hers, he likely wouldn't even see her much, other than at Katrina's reception.

She would be busy with the inn, with her photography, with her wide circle of friends, while he should be focused on finishing his manuscript and allowing his shoulder to heal—not to mention figuring out whether he would still have a career at the end of that time.

*Don't miss* THE COTTAGES ON SILVER BEACH
*by RaeAnne Thayne,*
*available July 2018*
*wherever HQN books and ebooks are sold!*

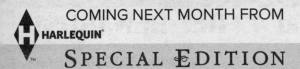

# COMING NEXT MONTH FROM

**HARLEQUIN®**

## SPECIAL EDITION

### Available July 17, 2018

#### #2635 THE MAVERICK'S BABY-IN-WAITING
*Montana Mavericks: The Lonelyhearts Ranch* • by Melissa Senate
After dumping her cheating fiancé, mom-to-be Mikayla Brown is trying to start fresh—without a man!—but Jensen Jones is determined to pursue her. He's not ready to be a daddy...or is he?

#### #2636 ADDING UP TO FAMILY
*Matchmaking Mamas* • by Marie Ferrarella
When widowed rocket scientist Steve Holder needs a housekeeper who can help with his precocious ten-year-old, The Matchmaking Mamas know just who to call! But Becky Reynolds soon finds herself in over her head—and on the path to gaining a family!

#### #2637 SHOW ME A HERO
*American Heroes* • by Allison Leigh
When small-town cop Ali Templeton shows up at Grant Cooper's door with a baby she says is his niece, the air force vet turned thriller writer is surprised by more than the baby—there's an undeniable attraction to deal with, too. Can he be a hero for more than just the baby's sake? Or will Ali be left out in the cold once again?

#### #2638 THE BACHELOR'S BABY SURPRISE
*Wilde Hearts* • by Teri Wilson
After a bad breakup and a one-night stand, Evangeline Holly just wants to forget the whole thing. But it turns out Ryan Wilde is NYC's hottest bachelor, her new boss—and the father of her child!

#### #2639 HER LOST AND FOUND BABY
*The Daycare Chronicles* • by Tara Taylor Quinn
Tabitha Jones has teamed up with her food-truck-running neighbor, Johnny Brubaker, to travel to different cities to find her missing son. But as they get closer to bringing Jackson back, they have to decide if they really want their time together to come to an end...

#### #2640 HIGH COUNTRY COWGIRL
*The Brands of Montana* • by Joanna Sims
Bonita Delafuente has deferred her dreams to care for her mother. Is falling for Gabe Brand going to force her to choose between love and medical school? Or will her medical history make the choice for her?

---

# Get 4 FREE REWARDS!

## We'll send you 2 FREE Books plus 2 FREE Mystery Gifts.

**Harlequin® Special Edition** books feature heroines finding the balance between their work life and personal life on the way to finding true love.

FREE
Value Over
$20

---

SPECIAL EXCERPT FROM

**H** HARLEQUIN®

# SPECIAL EDITION

*When small-town cop Ali Templeton finds the uncle
of an abandoned infant, she wasn't expecting a
famous author—or an undeniable attraction!*

*Read on for a sneak preview of
the next book in the **AMERICAN HEROES** miniseries,
SHOW ME A HERO,
by* New York Times *bestselling author Allison Leigh.*

"Are you going to ask when you can meet your niece?"

Grant grimaced. "You don't know that she's my niece.
You only think she is."

"It's a pretty good hunch," Ali continued. "If you're
willing to provide a DNA sample, we could know for
sure."

His DNA wouldn't prove squat, though he had no
intention of telling her that. Particularly now that they'd
become the focus of everyone inside the bar. The town
had a whopping population of 5,000. Maybe. It was
small, but that didn't mean there wasn't a chance he'd be
recognized. And the last thing he wanted was a rabid fan
showing up on his doorstep.

He'd had too much of that already. It was one of the
reasons he'd taken refuge at the ranch that his biological
grandparents had once owned. He'd picked it up for a
song when it was auctioned off years ago, but he hadn't
seriously entertained doing much of anything with it—
especially living there himself.

At the time, he'd just taken perverse pleasure in being able to buy up the place where he'd never been welcomed while they'd been alive.

Now it was in such bad disrepair that to stay there even temporarily, he'd been forced to make it habitable.

He wondered if Karen had stayed there, unbeknownst to him. If she was responsible for any of the graffiti or the holes in the walls.

He pushed away the thought and focused on the officer. "Ali. What's it short for?"

She hesitated, obviously caught off guard. "Alicia, but nobody ever calls me that." He'd been edging closer to the door, but she'd edged right along with him. "So, about that—"

Her first name hadn't been on the business card she'd left for him. "Ali fits you better than Alicia."

She gave him a look from beneath her just-from-bed sexy bangs. "Stop changing the subject, Mr. Cooper."

"Start talking about something else, then. Better yet—" he gestured toward the bar and Marty "—start doing the job you've gotta be getting paid for since I can't imagine you slinging drinks just for the hell of it."

Her eyes narrowed and her lips thinned. "Mr. Cooper—"

"G'night, Officer Ali." He pushed open the door and headed out into the night.

*Don't miss*
*SHOW ME A HERO by Allison Leigh,*
*available August 2018 wherever*
*Harlequin® Special Edition books and ebooks are sold.*

www.Harlequin.com